"You're supposed to be in bed, Molly, not sitting at my desk."

Justin tossed down the leather backpack he used as a combination medical bag and briefcase.

Molly. Molly. Molly. Sara repeated the name over and over in her mind, willing herself to think of it as her own.

"I'm going a little stir crazy," she admitted. "And I thought the clinic could use some help. You have no organizational skills."

"Guilty," he agreed easily.

Sara averted her eyes, afraid some of her lecherous thoughts might be evident in her expression. Getting a grip on her feelings for the handsome doctor was part of her new plan.

"I'm setting up an interface and configuring a single-use station for you." She reached out and adjusted the screen so Justin could see it more clearly. "You have all the tools right here, you just haven't been using them effectively."

"The story of my life," he commented wryly.

Sara was left wondering if that was some kind of double entendre, hoping maybe it was.

Dear Reader,

The Best Man in Texas was a wonderful opportunity to work with an incredible group of authors and editors! It is always a joy and an honor to be offered the chance to work with a terrific team.

Writing about Texas was great fun and it gave me a chance to reminisce about a trip my husband and I took to the state in 1985. We traveled through much of the diverse landscape and ended up at a dude ranch. Well, actually, it was more like a dude resort. We had a cabin with a hot tub, fireplace and a butler, so I doubt I can claim to have experienced true Western living. The butler was a nice touch, though.

Sara Pierce was a challenging character to develop. Though I could never imagine the true horrors of living through an abusive marriage, I fully enjoyed creating a woman who had not only survived, but had taken control of her life. What better reward than to find a true hero at the end of the journey. Dr. Justin Dale embodied all the qualities that make being a writer such a marvelous job. Crafting the hero is—secretly—my favorite part of the writing process. I'll admit, Justin is my ideal fantasy man—gorgeous, intelligent, morally grounded and genuinely kind.

And Justin has many things in common with my husband. Acknowledging the similarity makes me remember why I wanted to write romance. I not only believe in "happily ever after," I'm lucky enough to have found it in my own life as my husband and I prepare to celebrate twenty years of marriage.

I hope you enjoy the book, and please let me know what you think! You can write to me in care of Harlequin Books, 300 East 42nd Street, 6th Floor, New York, NY 10014. Or if you prefer electronic contact, visit www.KelseyRoberts.com.

Happy reading!

Kelsey Roberts

TRUEBLOOD, TEXAS

Kelsey Roberts

The Best Man in Texas

HARLEQUIN®

TORONTO • NEW YORK • LONDON
AMSTERDAM • PARIS • SYDNEY • HAMBURG
STOCKHOLM • ATHENS • TOKYO • MILAN • MADRID
PRAGUE • WARSAW • BUDAPEST • AUCKLAND

Kelsey Roberts is acknowledged as the author of this work.

Words simply cannot express my gratitude to my supportive and loving husband, Bob, my dear friends, my sister, Linda, the caring readers, patient editors and members of the writing community for their overwhelming support when I lost my son. Without all of you, I could easily have lost my way. Thank you!

In loving memory of Kyle McKinley Pollero
(November 19, 1985–September 7, 1999)

HARLEQUIN BOOKS
225 Duncan Mill Road, Don Mills,
Ontario, Canada M3B 3K9

ISBN-13: 978-0-373-65083-5
ISBN-10: 0-373-65083-3

THE BEST MAN IN TEXAS

TRUEBLOOD, TEXAS

THE TRUEBLOOD LEGACY

THE YEAR WAS 1918, and the Great War in Europe still raged, but Esau Porter was heading home to Texas.

The young sergeant arrived at his parents' ranch northwest of San Antonio on a Sunday night, only the celebration didn't go off as planned. Most of the townsfolk of Carmelita had come out to welcome Esau home, but when they saw the sorry condition of the boy, they gave their respects quickly and left.

The fever got so bad so fast that Mrs. Porter hardly knew what to do. By Monday night, before the doctor from San Antonio made it into town, Esau was dead.

The Porter family grieved. How could their son have survived the German peril, only to burn up and die in his own bed? It wasn't much of a surprise when Mrs. Porter took to her bed on Wednesday. But it was a hell of a shock when half the residents of Carmelita came down with the horrible illness. House after house was hit by death, and all the townspeople could do was pray for salvation.

None came. By the end of the year, over one hundred souls had perished. The influenza virus took those in the prime of life, leaving behind an unprecedented number of orphans. And the virus knew no boundaries. By the time the threat had passed, more than thirty-seven million people had succumbed worldwide.

But in one house, there was still hope.

Isabella Trueblood had come to Carmelita in the late 1800s with her father, blacksmith Saul Trueblood, and her mother, Teresa Collier Trueblood. The family had traveled from Indiana, leaving their Quaker roots behind.

Young Isabella grew up to be an intelligent woman who had a gift for healing and storytelling. Her dreams centered on the boy next door, Foster Carter, the son of Chester and Grace.

Just before the bad times came in 1918, Foster asked Isabella to be his wife, and the future of the Carter spread was secured. It was a happy union, and the future looked bright for the young couple.

Two years later, not one of their relatives was alive. How the young couple had survived was a miracle. And during the epidemic, Isabella and Foster had taken in more than twenty-two orphaned children from all over the county. They fed them, clothed them, taught them as if they were blood kin.

Then Isabella became pregnant, but there were complications. Love for her handsome son, Josiah, born in 1920, wasn't enough to stop her from growing weaker by the day. Knowing she couldn't leave her husband to tend to all the children if she died, she set out to find families for each one of her orphaned charges.

And so the Trueblood Foundation was born. Named in memory of Isabella's parents, it would become famous all over Texas. Some of the orphaned children went to strangers, but many were reunited with their families. After reading notices in newspapers and church bulletins, aunts, uncles, cousins and grandparents rushed to Carmelita to find the young ones they'd given up for dead.

Toward the end of Isabella's life, she'd brought together more than thirty families, and not just her orphans. Many others, old and young, made their way to her doorstep, and Isabella turned no one away.

At her death, the town's name was changed to Trueblood, in her honor. For years to come, her simple grave was adorned with flowers on the anniversary of her death, grateful tokens of appreciation from the families she had brought together.

Isabella's son, Josiah, grew into a fine rancher and married Rebecca Montgomery in 1938. They had a daughter, Elizabeth Trueblood Carter, in 1940. Elizabeth married her neighbor William Garrett in 1965, and gave birth to twins Lily and Dylan in 1971, and daughter Ashley a few years later. Home was the Double G ranch, about ten miles from Trueblood proper, and the Garrett children grew up listening to stories of their famous great-grandmother, Isabella. Because they were Truebloods, they knew that they, too, had a sacred duty to carry on the tradition passed down to them: finding lost souls and reuniting loved ones.

PROLOGUE

"HE'S GOING to kill you."

Ignoring the weave of tubes and electrodes, Violet Mitchum shifted on the gurney so she could peer through the small opening where the well-worn emergency room curtains didn't quite meet.

Breath snagged in her throat when she caught sight of the woman lying almost close enough for her to touch. Through the small opening in the privacy curtain, Violet was easily able to catalog the young woman's injuries. Beneath the raw, battered face, she suspected the woman was attractive. Though blood matted the long, pale-brown hair and the woman's clothes were torn, Violet was quite certain this was not a homeless person or woman forced to sell herself on the street.

What was left of her clothing indicated that, whoever she was, she took an effort in her appearance on a limited budget. There were traces of expertly applied makeup on and around the welts and abrasions marring her face.

"I know that," she heard the young woman reply wearily. She winced and held tentative fingertips to her rapidly swelling lip.

The attending physician rolled a stool next to the bed. His actions were so smooth from obvious repetition that they resembled an eerie kind of choreography. He was looking down at his patient with what Violet could only classify as frustrated compassion. That sentiment was echoed in his tone.

"Sara," he began on a rush of air, "let me call the cops. Hank Allen deserves—"

"To rot in hell," the woman named Sara finished with a spark of forced humor. "I'm taking care of it, Dr. Greene."

Violet watched as all pretext of professional distance drained from the doctor's face. "Really? How?"

"He didn't *mean* to hurt me," the woman replied with tenacious conviction. "Besides, he never would have hit me tonight if I hadn't mouthed off at him first. You've known me most of my life, Dr. Greene. I've never been very good at keeping my smart remarks to myself."

Violet stifled the urge to scoff.

"That hardly justifies Hank Allen beating you, Sara."

She attempted a grin in spite of her puffy upper lip. "I've got it under control," she insisted.

"Really?" the doctor challenged. "I've been hearing that same tune for the past three years. You're a young, intelligent woman, Sara. Why you stay with a husband who beats you makes no sense."

The young woman broke eye contact with the concerned physician.

"I married him, Dr. Greene. I can't just walk away from a commitment."

"You're right," the doctor agreed with more than just a measure of disgust. "A few more like tonight and you won't be walking away. They'll be carrying you out in a body bag."

Violet was distracted for the better part of an hour while a physician's assistant sutured her finger. She felt rather silly about the whole matter. She had come to Louisiana to help her friend Betty recuperate from a hip replacement. And here she was in an emergency room getting stitches because she had not been paying attention while chopping carrots. It seemed an inconsequential injury when compared with the poor girl in the next room.

Violet thought of her own wonderful marriage and couldn't fathom the life of the young woman in the nearby bed. Violet had been loved—no, cherished. *That* was marriage.

"Excuse me?" Violet began rather cautiously as she yanked open the flimsy curtain.

Gingerly, the young woman half turned on her side, angling herself so as to get a clear look at Violet through the less swollen of her two eyes. Violet's initial assessment had been accurate. Beneath her injuries, this woman was stunning. Except for the torment marring those beautiful brown eyes.

The young woman surprised her when she asked, "Do you need help? Should I call the nurse?"

Interesting, Violet thought, that this Sara should be concerned with her when she was clearly in a more serious condition herself.

Violet used her good hand to smooth back a few strands of her hair. It had long ago gone white and she hoped that alone was enough to lend some credence to what she was about to say.

"No, no," Violet assured her. "I'm simply awaiting a release from the doctor." She held up her now bandaged hand and turned it as if to prove it functioned.

"Me, too," she responded on a slightly labored breath.

Never one to mince words, Violet met and held the woman's gaze. "Your name is Sara, right?"

The woman nodded.

"I suppose you're going to go back to the man who did this to you?"

Sara's lids fluttered to shroud her eyes. "Do you always listen in on confidential conversations?"

Spirit, Violet thought. *Good sign.* "Only when I think I can help."

"You can't," came Sara's rote-sounding reply. "Anyway, I don't need anyone's help."

Stubbornness. Bad sign. "Your face and your ribs will heal but the problem with your husband won't," Violet continued, undeterred. "The doctors can fix your body but only you can fix your life."

"With all due respect, ma'am, you don't know me and you don't know my husband."

"I don't have to," Violet countered. "I know his type. But I'll admit that you're something of a puzzle. You seem like a bright, articulate woman. Smart enough to know better than to let a man use you as a punching bag."

Sara shifted onto her back and Violet thought she saw a shimmer of unshed tears in the woman's eyes. Violet wasn't sure if the woman's emotional control was a good or bad sign.

"You don't understand," Sara said after a brief silence.

"So explain it to me," Violet challenged.

"Hank Allen is under a lot of pressure. He owns several businesses and sometimes the stress just gets to him."

"You think that justifies beating you?"

"He wasn't always like this," Sara defended without real emotion. "He doesn't mean to get so rough." She continued to stare at the ceiling.

Violet guessed the practiced excuses were wearing thin even to Sara. "They never are. Batterers are successful because they start out as Prince Charming and wait until later to reveal their warts. And just for your information, warts can be removed for a while, but they usually grow back."

"I think he really wants to change this time."

"Is that what you thought all the other times?"

"It doesn't matter," Sara said, closing her eyes. "Marriage is a lifelong commitment."

"Only when it's made honestly," Violet counseled. "When your Hank Allen stood in front of God and promised to love and honor you 'till death do you part,' he was lying. Seems to me your commitment was based on false promises."

"I can't leave him," Sara said. "I have absolutely no money, no assets. I tried to leave once."

"What happened?"

"Hank Allen reported the car stolen. Everything is in his name. I'm not even authorized to write a check."

"There are places that can help you. Organizations that—"

"He'd find me."

Violet thought about her next move for less than a minute. "Let me help."

Sara's eyes flew open and she jerked her head around—a motion that obviously caused her some pain. Wincing, she said, "You don't even know me. I can't let—"

"All the better," Violet interrupted. "I'll give you some money to get yourself away from this mess."

"He'll go crazy. Besides, I couldn't possibly take money from a total stranger."

"I'm Violet Mitchum from Pinto, Texas. There, now we aren't strangers."

"You know what I mean," Sara argued. "This isn't your problem. I'll deal with it, but thank you."

"There's a fine line between being stubborn and being stupid, Sara."

"I'm being neither," Sara said. "I'm being practical. When the time is right, I'll leave Hank Allen."

"But when that time comes, will you still be breathing?"

CHAPTER ONE

"I'M STILL breathing, Violet," Sara Pierce sighed as she sank lower against the stiff seat of the bus.

But Violet's wisdom delivered nearly four years earlier had stayed with Sara. The mere fact that she had been so hopeless as to inspire a virtual stranger to take pity on her in a hospital emergency room had been just the push Sara needed. It had taken her months of careful planning and three more beatings, but she had done it.

Each week she had siphoned cash from the grocery allowance Hank Allen grudgingly provided. Sara had packed her bag a few articles of clothing at a time. If he suspected, Hank Allen never let on, but she had lived in mortal fear that he would discover her plan.

He didn't. Eight months after that fortuitous meeting with Violet Mitchum in the Louisiana hospital, Sara Pierce had walked out on years of abuse.

After a few months in hiding, she had contacted an attorney and started the process of reclaiming her life.

She gave Hank Allen some parting gifts. First, there was a restraining order. When he violated that, Sara pressed charges and Hank Allen went to jail for six months. During his incarceration, she had obtained a divorce that included Hank Allen having to pay her rehabilitative alimony for three years. It seemed only fair that he support her while she returned to finish the college degree she had interrupted to marry that pig.

It seemed as if her life was back on track. She hadn't seen Hank Allen in more than a year. The alimony had ended a week earlier, the day before she had earned her degree. Sara was ready to begin a new life.

But Hank Allen wasn't finished with her yet.

She had returned from her graduation ceremony, stepped inside her apartment, and only wished she hadn't known what hit her. It took one blow for her to recognize the all-too-familiar feel of Hank Allen's fists.

She was convinced that he would have beaten her to death had it not been for the intervention of a neighbor.

Sara repositioned her travel bag on the seat beside her—she didn't want any traveling companion on this trip—and crouched behind the dated newspaper she was using to obscure her face.

It seemed rather creepy that she found herself staring at the obituary page. A San Antonio socialite named Eve Bishop was smiling back at her. The wealthy woman's death apparently warranted almost a quarter-page of the paper. If Hank Allen had been successful, Sara knew her death would have gone unnoticed. She would have been little more than a statistic.

I *was* a statistic! she thought with incredible frustration. But no more. She had Violet Mitchum to thank for that, which was exactly what she was about to do.

Thank her and ask for help. Sara had learned a lot in the past few years. First and foremost, she had learned that asking for help was sometimes the only way out of a bad situation. Violet's simple offer that night in the hospital had changed the course of Sara's life. Now she needed a little more sage advice to salvage what she had struggled so hard to achieve. She hadn't even bothered to phone Violet—after Hank Allen's reappearance, all she could think about was fleeing to safety.

Outside the bus window Sara could see the vast expanse of Texas roll by. Since Hank Allen had not dared show his face at the hospital that night four years ago, he had no idea who Violet was. Consequently, he wouldn't know to look for her in some small place called Pinto. Violet would help her. Sara just knew in her bones that the kindly old woman would help her think of something. Some way to keep Hank Allen out of her life for good.

Sara shifted in the seat. The action caused her bruised ribs to smart. At least it was getting dark now. Dark enough that she no longer had to hide her battered face behind the newspaper. If the other riders noticed her bruises, they gave no outward indication.

She spotted the sign for Pinto outside the window. It made her feel safe. As an added measure of security, Sara remained on the bus until its next scheduled stop in Cactus Creek, a neighboring town. She wasn't taking any chances this time. This time her plan would work.

No one seemed to notice when she gathered her single bag and exited the bus in the center of Cactus Creek.

"Center" was an accurate description. Cactus Creek appeared to have a main street and very little else. It was perfect. It was also fairly deserted. Aside from a diner, no light shone from the other shops dotting the dusty sidewalk.

Sara reached into her purse and pulled a tattered piece of paper from a side compartment. The writing was faded but still legible. Violet Mitchum had left her address for Sara that night—just in case. The message read "My door is always open."

"Let's hope that's true," Sara muttered as she walked toward the diner.

The tinkle of a bell greeted her when she pushed the door open, along with the twang of a popular country ballad. The place was deserted save for an attractive couple huddled in the end booth and a waitress seated at the Formica counter, engrossed in a paperback novel.

"Coffee?" the waitress asked without looking up from her book.

Sara would have loved some, but it was already

late and she wanted to get to Violet's as soon as possible. "I need to know how to get to—" she paused and read from the scrap of paper "—Harvester Lane in Pinto."

The waitress lifted her head, her brows drawn tightly together. "You sure?"

Sara nodded, careful to keep her face turned subtly in profile. It was easier than letting the waitress see her bruises and then having to come up with an explanation.

"Hell of a long walk, and nothing on Harvester but the Mitchum place," the waitress informed her on a sigh.

"Point me in the right direction and I'll be on my way," Sara urged. Out of habit, she glanced over her shoulder and scanned the street beyond the window. Seeing no sign of Hank Allen was reassuring.

Knowing she still feared him wasn't. Especially when she noted the couple sharing coffee. The woman had her back to Sara but the man was facing in her direction. He was dark and handsome, and the way he reached out and patted his companion's hand was telling. His action seemed to convey genuine compassion and kindness. Sara scoffed inwardly. Like she was an authority on men. Still, she lingered a minute on his thick, wavy brown hair and chocolate-colored eyes. His chiseled face was perfectly sculpted, right down to the slight cleft in his chin and a perfect dimple on his right cheek, which appeared when he flashed an understated smile. Sara knew she was exhausted if she was cataloguing a strange man's assets.

"Being as it's late," the waitress's voice intruded as she slipped behind the counter, "why don't I give you a cup of coffee—it's fresh—and point you in the direction of the boardinghouse."

Sara read the bright white nameplate pinned to the woman's tight blouse. "Thank you…Stella. But I really do need to be on my way."

Stella's dark eyes were probing as she hesitated, coffeepot in hand. Then, with an accepting shrug, she said, "Suit yourself. Go out the door, take a left and follow Main Street to the stop sign. Main runs right into FM 880. Harvester is on the right a few miles down. Just look for a lattice rose trellis. Can't miss it."

"Thanks," Sara muttered.

She left the Blue Moon Café and followed the simple directions. Simple, yes, easy, no. Everything in Texas *was* big, she determined as she continued to walk. Her small overnight bag felt as if it were filled with bricks and her feet weren't too thrilled as she trudged down the dark road.

As soon as she passed the stop sign, she felt she had crossed some unseen border. There was a freshness in the crisp, cool night air. She could hear birds or some kind of critters scuttling in the underbrush as she walked through the virgin, ankle-high grass along the edge of the road. Occasionally a twig snapped beneath her foot or she would stumble on a rock. Her ribs ached and sleep deprivation was catching up with her. These were the longest miles she had ever walked. Violet would be a welcome sight.

Sara spotted the rose trellis up ahead. It had a strangely neglected look about it, even in the darkness. The roses were slowly being strangled by the hearty climbing weed overtaking the trellis.

But then, Violet was older, Sara told herself as she walked up a crushed-stone drive. Perhaps she wasn't able to maintain the property any longer. Sara was already planning on weeding the rose bed and doing a little pruning when she reflexively ducked to the side and crouched down in the tall grass.

A car was coming.

Stifling the urge to cry out when her ribs protested, she clutched her bag close to her and listened. She saw the dual beams of headlights crawling along the main road. They were coming from the direction of town. Sara huddled lower in the grass, praying there were no snakes lurking nearby.

It seemed to take an eternity for the car to drive by the entrance to Violet's ranch.

Sara needed a good few minutes before she had the courage to come out of hiding. "Get a grip!" she admonished herself. "It was probably the couple from the diner going home." Unable to help herself, Sara started to create a scenario for the cute couple. What would it be like to have a real relationship with a man who looked like that!

She continued her musings as she headed toward the house. And then it happened.

With no time to run, she turned, dropping her bag to shield her eyes from the bright beams of the headlights that appeared out of nowhere before her. Her heart skipped several beats, making her chest feel as if it would explode. Fear replaced the blood flowing in her veins. This was her worst nightmare come true. She was in the middle of nowhere. Despite all her careful planning, she had provided her ex-husband with the perfect venue to kill her.

A spotlight clicked on from the driver's side of the car. Sara could feel heat from the light as the car inched closer. Something didn't seem right. Where had Hank Allen gotten a spotlight?

She was virtually blinded by the lights. An odd sense of calm washed over her. She ran the situation through her mind, remembering everything she had been taught in her self-defense course. *Cooperation,* she repeated like a mantra. *Don't antagonize him and don't get into the car!*

"Step up to the car, please, ma'am."

Sara blinked at the unfamiliar male voice. She remained frozen in place.

"Texas State Police, ma'am. Step up to the front of the vehicle and place your palms on the hood."

The disembodied voice was bellowing from a speaker. Sara was trying to grasp this sudden change in her situation when she heard a muffled curse as the car door opened.

"Lady," an irritated young officer groused, "would you come on over here, please?"

"What?"

"Geez!" the young man groaned as he moved toward her. "What happened to you?"

"What?" Sara repeated.

He emerged from the spotlight, his gun belt jingling with each step he took. The faint smell of aftershave arrived a split second before the young officer. Tipping the brim of his uniform hat back slightly, he stared down at her face with a frown.

"You need medical attention, ma'am."

Coming out of her fog, Sara gently shook her head. "No, I'm fine."

"You aren't fine," he argued. "Who did this to you and what are you doing out here in the middle of the night?"

"Visiting a friend," Sara explained.

His brows crunched together. "I don't think so," he countered. "If you tell me the truth, I can help you."

Sara didn't want to tell him how many times she had heard that before. There was the marriage counselor who was going to help her. Then the doctor who was going to help her. And the divorce attorney. And the support group. And the college dean. And the judge who issued the restraining order.

"Thank you, but I'm fine," she managed to reply as politely as possible.

"You aren't fine," he argued.

"My friend owns this place," Sara explained.

He snorted. "Is that right?"

"Yes. I'm surprised she hasn't come outside with all these lights shining." *Why hasn't she?* Sara wondered to herself.

"Is this friend Miss Violet?" the officer queried.

Sara nodded.

"She isn't here."

Sara felt her heart plummet. "Not here?"

"You say she's a friend?"

Sara nodded. "Yes, we met a few years ago."

"You couldn't have been too close," the officer said. "Miss Violet died a while back. Which means *you* are *trespassing*."

CHAPTER TWO

"IT WOULD BE a lot easier if you would just tell me your name," the trooper said for the fifth time during their ride.

"I've agreed to go to the Harrisons' shelter," Sara argued. "Believe me, it's better if no one knows my name."

"What about your kin?" he asked. "Isn't there someone you'd like me to call? Let them know you're okay?"

"I don't have anyone, but thank you."

"What kind of man did this to you?"

"The worst kind."

THE HARRISONS' shelter was a converted bunkhouse on an immaculate ranch just outside the town of Pinto. It was pitch-dark when Kathy Harrison greeted them at the locked gate in her bathrobe.

She offered Sara a warm smile, then placed her arm around her shoulders and steered her to the main house. Kathy dismissed the trooper, then insisted that Sara have something to eat.

"You want to tell me your name?" Kathy asked as she piled lettuce on a sandwich.

"Jane Doe?" Sara suggested. She clutched the steaming coffee in both hands.

Kathy chuckled and joined Sara at the spacious oak clawfoot table that dominated the cozy kitchen. "You don't look like a Jane."

Sara simply smiled. Her smile slipped a bit when an imposing man with white hair entered the kitchen.

"This is my husband, David," Kathy explained.

Sara's greeting was a tentative meeting of the eyes.

"I smelled sandwiches," David commented easily. Unlike his wife, he made no move to make physical contact. In fact, he seemed careful to avoid invading her space.

"I'm not really hungry," Sara insisted.

"You should eat," Kathy admonished.

"You should do what you want," David countered as he accepted the plate Sara had pushed toward the center of the table. "Kathy can be something of a mother hen."

"The girl looks half-starved," Kathy protested.

David took a hearty bite of the sandwich and ate with appreciation. On a routine obviously established over many years, Kathy provided her husband with a glass of milk and a familiar pat on the shoulder.

This was what a marriage was supposed to be, Sara thought.

David met her gaze and asked, "Are you going to make us keep calling you 'the girl?'"

Sara felt a little silly. Her face warmed with an

uncomfortable blush. "If you don't know my name, then you can't tell anyone about me."

"We don't tell," David stated with conviction. "This is a safe place. We've got an arrangement with law enforcement in four counties. They know if they bring a woman here for shelter, she'll be safe because we know better than to reveal information. We know how dangerous it is."

"I doubt it," Sara sighed.

Kathy disappeared and returned in a flash with a framed photograph. She handed it to Sara as if she were handing her a diamond-studded scepter. The young woman in the photograph was beautiful, with a smile that simply required you to return it in kind.

"That's our daughter Dorothy," Kathy explained.

"She's lovely."

Kathy nodded and her hand slipped into David's. "She was. She was beaten to death by her boyfriend ten years ago."

"I'm s-sorry."

David's smile was haunted now. "We do understand your situation. Dorothy is the reason we started this shelter. We know how important it is for women to have someplace safe to hide."

"Hiding isn't living," Sara sighed.

"It's better than the alternative," Kathy said.

Sara felt guilty for voicing her thoughts in light of what the Harrisons had just told her. "I don't think my ex-husband followed me," she said.

"What happened?"

Sara shrugged and ran her fingertip around the rim of her coffee mug. "He wasn't exactly proud of my graduation from college."

"When was this?"

A lifetime ago. "Two days ago," Sara answered. "I went back to college after my divorce. I worked hard and managed to finish midyear."

"Congratulations," David offered.

Amazingly, it was the first she had heard those words from anyone other than herself.

"Can we get you some medical attention as a graduation gift?"

Sara smiled at David's offer. "I'm fine," she insisted. "A few bruised ribs. I've had worse."

"Let us call Justin anyway," Kathy suggested.

"I'm on a limited budget," Sara countered.

"Justin doesn't charge anything," Kathy explained. "He's a good old-fashioned country doctor. Still makes house calls and is happy to accept a fresh-baked pie for his trouble."

"Thank you anyway," Sara insisted.

"You're as stubborn as the other one," David commented.

"The other one?"

"Came in just before dinner," David said. "Looks like the devil chewed her up and spit her out. I'm hoping she'll rethink things by morning."

"She's Jane Doe number one," Kathy explained. "It's going to be hard what with two Jane Does staying with us."

"I'm not staying," Sara said. "I'm sorry the state trooper insisted on bringing me here. He said it was either this or jail. Apparently I was trespassing."

"My guess is he knew you'd be safe here." Kathy took Sara's coffee mug to the sink. "Why don't you get some sleep? We'll see how things look to you in the light of day."

She was tired, Sara admitted, and she didn't have any alternative plan worked out. Not yet at least.

Kathy led her from the house to the adjacent bunkhouse. It had been outfitted with beds, dressers, sofas and chairs. There was a fireplace and someone—David probably—had gone to the trouble to enclose two nice bathrooms in the rectangular space.

The rows of single beds reminded Sara of her days in the orphanage. They were bittersweet memories. She had grieved for her parents but was loved by the staff.

Kathy showed her where the telephone was and told her she was free to call anyone, anywhere, anytime. Then she was led to a bed next to one occupied by a sleeping woman. In hushed tones, Kathy wished her good-night and left her to prepare for bed.

Sara washed up and quietly returned to her assigned bed. She had slipped beneath the covers when she heard the soft sobs.

"Are you okay?"

There was no answer.

Sara lay still for several minutes, listening to the

cries, before tossing off the blankets and padding over to the bedside of her only roommate.

Gently, she touched her on the shoulder. The woman was trembling and gulping air between sobs.

"I'm Sara," she said as she brushed the woman's hair away from her face. Sara didn't flinch when she saw the deep lacerations and dark bruises. It was difficult to get a true picture of the woman's face in its current condition. All Sara could tell was that they shared similar coloring and were probably close in age. "Let me help you. Do you want me to call Kathy?"

"No!" the woman answered in a panic. "I just want it to be over."

"It is," Sara assured her. "You're safe here."

"I'll never be safe," she replied, defeated. "Jeb will find me. He always does."

"You can't think that way," Sara insisted. "All you need is a plan."

The woman's sobs slowed and she turned to peer up at Sara with reddened, puffy eyes. "Did you have a plan?"

Sara nodded.

"Did you a lot of good, didn't it?"

Sara shrugged. "So I had a *flawed* plan. I won't make that mistake again. Look, um—"

"Molly," the woman provided in a near whisper.

"Look, Molly, you can't give up. You just have to think of a way to rebuild your life."

"I don't have a life."

"But you can," Sara insisted. "You can go some-place fresh, start a new life."

"I tried that."

"Then try again," Sara urged. "Don't let him win."

Molly was quiet for some time before she turned away and whispered, "He already has."

SARA WOKE a few hours later and didn't feel much better for the effort. Her brain was shrouded in a fog of exhaustion but she found sleep elusive. She needed a plan. She needed a new identity, one that Hank Allen couldn't track.

She recalled a TV movie where the character had gone to a cemetery and stolen the name and birthdate of a deceased person around the same age. Then, us-ing that information, she had gotten a birth certificate. Sara could do the same. With a birth certificate, she could get a Social Security card, then a driver's li-cense. The only problem would be where to hide and how to support herself while she was creating her new self. She supposed she could stay with the Harrisons, though that could be problematic. The trooper had probably filled out a report. If Hank Allen knew she took the bus from Louisiana to Texas, he would even-tually find the report and put two and two together. No, Sara needed a clean break. No trail to cover, no loose ends.

She glanced over and saw that Molly was sleeping. Quietly, Sara crept from the bed over to the telephone

stand. Despite a brief search, she couldn't find a telephone book. She wanted to see if there were any cem-
eteries listed in the area. Careful not to disturb Molly,
Sara looked around the rest of the bunkhouse. Still
no phone book. Maybe Molly knew where it was.

She glanced over her shoulder. Molly still hadn't
moved. Sara was in a quandary. Her roommate
needed rest, but Sara was feeling desperate to get
started on her new life. She reasoned that if she awak-
ened Molly, she could apologize by helping her make
her own fresh start.

Sara walked over to the bed and gently shook
Molly's shoulder. The motion caused Molly's arm to
fall from the bed. Sara heard something hit the floor.
It rolled over and brushed against her foot.

Reaching down, Sara picked up the small, opaque-
orange plastic bottle. The cap was missing. Holding
it up to the sliver of daylight just entering the room,
she read the label.

"Molly Parker. Diazepam. Take two at bedtime."
The prescription had been filled at a pharmacy in
Austin two days earlier. Originally, there were sixty
pills in the bottle. Assuming Molly had taken the pre-
scribed dose, there should have been fifty-six left.
There were none.

"Oh, God!" Sara breathed in panic. Yanking away
the covers, she felt for a pulse.

Not only did Molly not have a pulse, her body was
cold and lifeless. After spending two years working

part-time in a hospital emergency room, Sara knew a dead body when she saw one.

"You didn't have to do this," she said to Molly. "This means he won. Damn it!"

Sara turned to go and get the Harrisons, but her foot caught a strap beneath the bed. When she went to untangle herself, she discovered she was hooked on Molly's purse.

The idea came to her at the same second she reached for the purse. There was enough of a resemblance...she hoped.

Silently she weighed the pros and cons. She'd be taking on Molly's problems as her own. She'd be cheating Molly's family—assuming she had one—out of grieving for her. In exchange, Sara would be getting Hank Allen out of her life forever. He'd be notified of her suicide and stop looking for her. Worst case scenario would be that Molly's abuser would come looking for her, but he'd be looking for Molly. Even if he found Sara, he most likely wouldn't do anything. Men who abused their wives and girlfriends normally didn't attack total strangers.

It could work. She could go back and hide out in Violet's house until her injuries healed. If someone was looking for Molly Parker, they wouldn't look on Harvester Lane.

It had to work. Her life depended on it.

Sara opened Molly's purse and started to go through the contents. She was relieved when she found no pictures of children. It would be impossible to steal the woman's identity if there were children involved.

She felt a pang of guilt when she came across a picture of a couple she assumed were Molly's parents. She found a driver's license and other identification. The two of them looked close enough alike to fool most people. Molly was an inch taller, but Sara doubted that would pose a problem. She was also a year younger.

That realization gave Sara pause. Molly had had only twenty-four years of life. It was senseless. Criminal.

It was also getting light outside.

Sara needed to get out while she could. Going to the phone, she wanted to call for a cab but doubted there were anything in such a place. It didn't matter. She knew Violet's house was to the west. She also knew the bus traveled the main road.

Carefully, Sara switched clothing with Molly, then placed the woman's lifeless body in the bed Kathy Harrison had assigned to her hours before. It was a gruesome task, but necessary. It was self-preservation.

"Thank you," Sara whispered as she put Molly's purse on her shoulder and left her own on the floor beside her travel bag. "Rest in peace, Sara Pierce." Without another word, she slipped out in to the dawn.

She had to climb over the fence in order to exit the Harrisons' ranch. It didn't do much for her ribs, but Sara wasn't about to let that foil her plan. After dropping to the ground, she headed down the main road, constantly glancing over her shoulder. She fully expected one of the Harrisons to discover what she had done and come after her.

She walked for more than an hour before the first car passed by. Apparently this wasn't the most heavily traveled road in Texas. Sara was tired and starting to question her judgment when a second car drove past, then stopped and waited as she caught up.

An elderly woman with a ready smile sat behind the wheel. "You lost, child?"

Sara shook her head. "I got off the bus in the wrong town."

If the woman noticed her bruises, she didn't let on. "You aren't from around here, are you?"

"No, ma'am."

"I knew it," she said with an exaggerated sigh. "No self-respecting woman from Texas would be fool enough to set out on foot. Get in."

"I don't want to be a bother."

"Then don't argue with me," she said. "Arguing bothers me. I can take you as far as Fort Worth."

Sara settled into the ancient automobile. It felt good to be off her feet. "Thank you. But I only need to go as far as the edge of town."

"What's your name?"

"Parker. Um, Molly Parker."

The woman shot her a quick glance. "You sure?"

Sara's heart stopped. "Y-yes."

"Okay. But it sounded like you were trying the name out for the very first time."

Molly Parker. Molly Parker. Molly Parker. Sara practiced the name in her head. She sat quietly until she spotted the wilting roses at the entrance to Violet's ranch.

The woman refused any offer of payment for gas when Sara stepped from the car. She simply smiled and gunned the old sedan on its way.

Sara started to cross the road when she heard the roar of an engine behind her. She looked up a split second before the car slammed into her body.

CHAPTER THREE

"MOLLY? Miss Parker?"

It took a herculean effort for her to open her eyes. The instant she did, she closed them because the bright, fluorescent light caused a pulsating pain in her head. While she was on the subject of pain, her ankle was throbbing as well.

"Miss Parker? Open your eyes for me again."

Reluctantly, she did as instructed. Blinking several times, she began to take in the unfamiliar surroundings. She smelled alcohol and antiseptic. She was wearing a thin cotton gown and was lying on a bed covered with a paper drape. Just a slight movement of her arm caused the paper to crunch several decibels too high.

Finally, she met the intense gaze of the speaker. He loomed above her, even though he appeared to be seated on a chair or a stool at her bedside. His eyes were rich brown—the color of designer coffee. His hair was also brown, and thick and ruffled, as though he'd raked his fingers through it just recently. There was a subtle cleft in his chin, just above where he had loosened the knot on his tie.

Beneath his suit jacket, she could see a well-worn

denim shirt. And shoulders that seemed to go on forever. Apparently she hadn't injured her libido in the...in the...

"What happened?" she asked, sudden panic welling inside her. "Where am I?"

His response was a calming smile. The action caused a faint dimple to appear near his attractive mouth. "I'm Justin Dale and you're in my clinic in Cactus Creek, Miss Parker."

"I don't understand!"

"Calm down," he urged as he placed a hand on her forearm.

It tingled where he touched her. That was disconcerting, but not as disconcerting as the alarm sounding in her brain.

"I can't calm down," she insisted as she tried to rise.

Gently but firmly, Justin stopped her. Something wasn't quite right. He could see it in her eyes. "You've got a broken ankle that I need to set," he explained. "Lie still so I can do an assessment. You've been waffling in and out of consciousness for quite a while since you were found at the accident scene."

She looked up at him. Her brown eyes were thickly lashed and golden starbursts radiated from her pupils. He chastised himself for noticing something so unprofessional. He was supposed to note that her pupils were equal and reactive, not incredibly beautiful. *Man, I've been too long without a date,* he thought.

"Forget my ankle!" she insisted.

Her voice was deep and a touch on the husky side. In spite of the fact that she'd been beaten and hit by a car, this woman still managed to exude a subtle kind of sensuality that he had neither expected nor—apparently—prepared for.

"I'm a doctor. I'm not allowed to forget fractures, Miss Parker."

"Who is Miss Parker?" she demanded urgently.

Justin had been in the middle of checking her pulse when he went still. "Excuse me?"

He saw a flash of emotion—anger or frustration or both—in her expression.

"Am I Molly Parker?"

Justin whipped out his penlight and again checked her pupils. He forced his tone to be placid as he asked, "Are you telling me you don't remember your name?"

She swatted the penlight away from her face. "I'm telling you I don't remember *anything*."

Taking in a deep breath, Justin pulled back and ran several possibilities through his mind. "Concussion can often result in short-term memory interruption. What is the last thing you can remember?"

"Waking up here."

He scratched the side of his neck. "I think it would be a good idea for me to set your ankle then transport you to the hospital in Fort Worth."

"No!"

Justin was startled by her urgent reaction. "The

hospital is better equipped to deal with a major head trauma and—''

She cut him off by gripping the sleeve of his jacket. "Please don't send me anywhere. I don't know why, but I just have this feeling that I'm safe here. That doesn't make sense, does it?" She lowered her eyes and nervously drew her lower lip between her teeth.

"It makes perfect sense," he assured her. "Your ankle isn't your only injury. You obviously took a hit to the head, and X rays showed you have a small crack in one of your ribs in addition to—''

"You said I was in an accident?" she interrupted him.

He nodded. "You were hit by a car. But that isn't what cracked your rib or caused most of the lacerations and hematomas to your face."

"What?"

"Doctor talk for cuts and bruises. My guess is they're two to three days old."

"I was in a fight *and* a car accident? What kind of person am I?"

"Probably a very decent one," he hypothesized. "If it was a fight, it was one-sided. No offensive or defensive wounds on your knuckles. Most likely, you were the victim of a crime or—''

"Or what?"

"Domestic violence. Which, by the way, is a crime."

"Am I married?" She asked the question with abject horror in her tone.

He shrugged. "No wedding ring. No pictures in your wallet. You don't have to be married to someone to get beaten, Molly."

She rubbed her face with her hands. "I think I would have preferred it if you'd said I was in a barroom brawl."

He chuckled. Obviously this woman had maintained her sense of humor under horrific circumstances. It galled him to think of a man abusing any woman, particularly this one. She wasn't short, just petite. Fragile. What kind of animal would attack someone so physically defenseless? And why did he have an urge to scoop her into his arms?

Sobering, he said, "I should tell you the circumstances surrounding the accident."

"It gets worse?" she asked in a defeated voice.

"Pretty much. There were no witnesses, according to Sheriff Younger, and no skid marks at the scene."

"Meaning?"

"The driver who hit you was either seriously distracted or..."

"Or?"

"Or aiming for you."

MOLLY SPENT the following few minutes trying in vain to recall something—anything—but her memory had been erased like a chalkboard. It was too weird. She had no problem remembering who was president of the United States or how to format and configure a computer's hard drive, but everything personal had been selectively deleted.

Frustrated, she found herself searching the clinic for Dr. Dale, the one and only face that was familiar. He had gone to mix some plaster to make her cast. The clinic was small and rather homey looking—she counted six beds in her immediate area, someone had painted aquatic murals on two of the walls.

Molly pulled herself up to rest on her elbows in order to get a better view of the place. Peering around the curtain, she spotted an attractive brunette leaning over a crib. She could hear the woman singing softly and see small, chubby legs in the crib. The infant's bed was shrouded in some sort of plastic and a nearby machine made rhythmic whooshing sounds.

The woman turned then and caught Molly staring at her. It might have been awkward, but she simply reached inside the plastic cover, touched the baby and walked over to Molly.

"Hi. I'm Julie," she said upon arrival.

The woman looked on the verge of total exhaustion but her warm smile seemed genuine.

"I'm Molly Porter—um—Parker. Molly Parker." The name still felt foreign on her tongue.

Julie rubbed her neck and rolled her head as she apparently worked out some stiffness.

"Is that your baby?" Molly asked.

Julie nodded. "Thomas. He's finally turning the corner. I would have lost him to pneumonia if it hadn't been for Justin."

"Aside from miracles, I can also walk on water," Dr. Dale quipped with an easy grin as he brought a small basin and rolls of fiberglass tape to set her ankle.

Molly didn't recognize her own name but she sure recognized the pang of jealousy she felt when Julie gave the gorgeous doctor a familiar, playful shove. Maybe Molly had suffered brain damage after all. That was the only plausible explanation for feeling such an intimate emotion about a total stranger.

"This could be uncomfortable, but I'm reluctant to give you any pain medication that might cause drowsiness because of the concussion," he explained.

When his palm gently slid beneath her calf, Molly was pretty sure no sedative could have dulled the flood of sensation. His long, tapered fingers were warm where they gripped her flesh. She felt oddly flushed and was glad she was no longer connected to the blood-pressure monitor. Surely it would have registered her inappropriate and humiliating reaction to his touch.

Julie excused herself and returned to baby Thomas while Molly forced herself to stare at the ceiling. Looking at the doctor wasn't an option. Though she'd lost her memory, she was fairly sure that applying a cast was not supposed to be a turn-on. Lord, maybe she was some sort of slut!

No, she reasoned. If she were, she wouldn't be feeling the full weight of guilt seizing her chest.

Despite her best efforts to resist, she noticed that

he was well toned. Not muscle-bound, just incredibly fit. Her mind went into fantasyland when she postulated that beneath his soft shirt were broad shoulders, a tapered waist and sculpted abdominals. Her gaze darted to his legs for an instant, long enough to fuel her musings. His jeans were faded, well-worn, and she could clearly see the outline of defined thigh muscles.

The room seemed to be getting warmer by the second.

Carefully, he slipped some sort of cotton, open-toed, sock-thing over her foot. It went up her leg about five inches. It felt as if he spent a long weekend adjusting and readjusting the fabric. Molly no longer felt pain from the fracture. Instead, her mind was totally focused on the electric sensation of his determined and well-trained fingers. Each place his skin brushed hers, a tingle lingered.

She felt her face grow hot.

"Is this uncomfortable?" the doctor asked.

Big-time. But probably not in the way you mean. "Nope, not at all."

"You look flushed. This isn't supposed to be a test of your fortitude. I can give you something for the pain, if it's too bad," he suggested.

She simply shook her head, afraid if she tried to speak, her wayward thoughts would be betrayed in her tone. Besides, what she wasn't feeling was pain. It was a thrill, a rush of excitement ricocheting around in her stomach. She wasn't a doctor, but she was sure that her symptoms had nothing to do with any injury.

Obviously satisfied with the first step, he scooted the stool around and braced her injured left foot against his chest.

"This might be uncomfortable," he warned casually.

But there was nothing casual about the feel of his solid chest beneath her foot. She was aware of its systematic rising and falling as he breathed steadily, in and out. Conversely, her breath was were coming in shallow near gasps.

With slow deliberation, Dr. Dale began to wrap her foot and ankle in cool, wet fiberglass. Every time he stroked and smoothed the wrap, her heart fluttered. Molly was awash in conflicting emotions and a sense of self-loathing.

He was merely doing his job and she was mentally turning it into some sort of torrid moment. Her eyes were riveted to his handsome profile. The man's face was an attractive combination of sharp angles and expressive compassion. Deep lines formed at the corners of his chocolate eyes as he continued his task.

Molly tried to redirect her thinking by glancing over at Julie and her baby. Apparently the baby was sleeping because Julie was seated, reading *The Collected Poems of Dylan Thomas*.

Depressing reading, Molly thought. At the same instant, she heard selected passages of Thomas in her head. That meant she was either educated or well-read.

"Is that frown due to pain?" the doctor asked, startling her.

Molly shook her head. "I know Thomas."

"The baby?" he asked, crooking his head toward the sleeping infant.

"The poet."

Justin dazzled her with a wry smile. The flash of perfectly straight white teeth was accompanied by a glimpse of his very sexy dimple.

Molly struggled to keep her thoughts on task. "If I know poetry, that must mean *something*."

"Yeah," he said as he applied the final touches to her cast. "It means, unlike me, you have the ability to understand poems that don't rhyme."

She found herself smiling. "It *is* something, isn't it?"

Justin met her eyes and held them. "Yes, it's a good sign. It most likely means that your amnesia is a temporary reaction to the trauma you suffered. You should expect to get snippets of memory, then most things will come back in time."

"In time? And what do you mean, 'most things'?"

He patted her hand. "I wouldn't be surprised if you never regain a clear memory of the accident. It's your brain's way of protecting you."

Molly stared, stunned. "How am I supposed to know what happened to me?"

He shrugged. "You'll probably never know unless they find the driver or a witness."

"Great! I'd really like to know if someone was just irresponsible or trying to hurt me."

"My educated guess is the latter. I don't think it's coincidence that you were beaten and hit by a car in the same week."

"You have no idea how *not* comforting that is."

A man in uniform stepped into the clinic just then. He greeted Julie in passing as he came over to where Molly was still stuck on her paper-covered bed.

Tipping the brim of his hat to her, he first addressed the doctor. "How's the patient?"

"Um...forgetful?" he suggested with a sheepish wink in Molly's direction.

"Sheriff Alec Younger," he introduced. "I need to get some information, if you're up to it, ma'am."

"You won't need a pencil," Molly quipped.

Her joke was lost on the sheriff. "Ma'am?"

She looked at Justin, silently conveying that she would prefer him to supply an explanation for her strange circumstance.

He picked up on her unspoken need immediately. "Physically, I've done everything possible, but there's a hitch."

"Hitch?" the sheriff asked.

"There's been a slight, probably short-term complication from the concussion she suffered."

"You moving her to Fort Worth?"

Justin shook his head. "I don't think that's necessary."

The sheriff rubbed the shadow of a beard on his chin. "So what exactly is this hitch?"

"Memory disruption."

"Come again?" Sheriff Younger pressed.

"More commonly known as amnesia."

The sheriff's dark brows drew together. "Is this a joke, Justin? I'm not really in the mood for games. I was late getting here because of a suicide in Pinto."

"You don't have jurisdiction in Pinto," Justin said.

"The Pinto suicide is related to *this* investigation," Sheriff Younger explained. "I got a call from the Harrisons."

"How are Kathy and David?" Justin asked.

Molly felt as if she were watching a Ping-Pong match. Couldn't these guys stick to one topic of conversation?

"Bummed," the sheriff answered. "They had a runner last night, then woke up this morning to find their latest guest had committed suicide."

"I hope you aren't talking about a hotel," Molly said.

"The Harrisons run a shelter," Justin explained, but his attention remained fixed on the sheriff. "So what does the suicide have to do with Molly getting hit by a car?"

"I'll get to that," the sheriff answered. He moved slightly closer to Molly and his piercing black eyes met hers. "I ran your name through our computer."

Molly stilled, curious, anxious and panicked all at the same instant. "Am I in trouble?"

He shrugged. "Nothing came back. Not in this county, at least. Where are you from?"

"I don't know."

The sheriff looked annoyed. "This is serious, young lady. This isn't a time for faking."

"I'm not faking!" Molly insisted rather haughtily. "I honestly can't remember."

Sheriff Younger turned to Justin. "This is a pretty big hitch."

"Yep."

"Great. Well, you had a Texas license, Austin address. I'll run a check there." The sheriff turned as if to leave.

"Wait!" Molly grabbed his sleeve. "I think I need help."

"She's right," Justin added. "I found some old injuries." He went on to detail the results of his physical examination.

The sheriff took some time absorbing the information, then said, "Well, that might fit with what I learned at the Harrisons."

"Which was?" Justin queried.

"That Ms. Parker is their runner. But there's a problem."

"Problem?" Molly repeated.

"Yep. The woman who committed suicide at the shelter last night was a woman named Sara Pierce."

"What does that have to do with Molly?" Justin pressed.

"She killed herself with an overdose of prescription drugs."

"Unfortunately a common means of ending one's life," Justin offered.

"Sure," the sheriff said, speaking directly to Molly, "but the prescription belonged to *you*."

CHAPTER FOUR

"So, AM I like a suspect or something?"

The sheriff shrugged. "Depends on the results of the Pierce woman's autopsy."

Molly felt an odd sensation. It was like a flashbulb going off in her mind. It was so quick she couldn't hold the image.

"Are you okay?" Justin asked as he took her hand in his. In one fluid motion he had managed to shove the sheriff off to the side to give her his full attention.

"Y-yes." Molly rubbed her palm across her forehead. "I just blanked for a minute."

Justin turned to the sheriff and said, "Alec, maybe now isn't a good time for this."

"I'll be back."

The sheriff's proclamation did little to calm Molly's frazzled state. Who were the Harrisons? Who was Sara Pierce and what did any of them have to do with her?

Without dropping her hand, Justin pulled his stool to the edge of her bed and lowered his more than six-foot frame onto it. "Don't make yourself crazy, Molly. Just relax and things will probably fall into place."

She felt herself frown. *"Probably?"*

Justin treated her to a handsome grin. "Worrying won't alter the outcome," he said.

She watched, transfixed, as his gaze dropped to their entwined hands. Once realization struck, he snatched his hand away, then all but tucked it behind his sizeable frame.

"I've got to check on the baby before Mrs. Beasley comes in."

Abruptly, Justin walked away. Molly said nothing. She was occupied taking in the sight of his broad back, incredible tush and slight swagger. It seemed more likely than not that Justin was perplexed. And she didn't think it was because of her condition. Had he been feeling the same energy that heated the pit of her stomach?

"The same energy?" Molly groused softly as she threw her arm over her face. "Is lust a form of energy?"

"It can be."

Molly shot upright when she heard the response to her very rhetorical and very private question.

Julie was standing next to the bed with a pitcher, a glass and a lecherous smile. "Justin thought you might be thirsty." She placed the beverage on the side table and pulled the stool over. "If you're going to lust after Justin, be prepared to stand in line."

Molly felt her cheeks burn. "I hardly know him, I—I—"

"Wouldn't be normal if you didn't notice he's gorgeous, smart, kind, compassionate *and* sexy as hell," Julie finished in a conspiratorial tone.

Molly thought for a second, then said, "Have I just stepped on your toes?"

Tossing her head back, Julie laughed softly. "Me? The only man in my life is Thomas."

"His father?" Molly asked.

"Has never even seen him. If I have anything to say about it, my husband won't ever be a part of Thomas's life."

"I guess that gives us something in common," Molly sighed. "Whatever man I was involved with beat me up, too, according to Justin."

"My husband never hit me," Julie corrected, an intense sadness creeping into her eyes. It was a pained, haunted expression.

"I didn't mean to jump to conclusions," Molly said. "Besides, it really isn't any of my business."

Julie shrugged. "You're the first person I've talked to like this in months. It helps."

"Feel free to use me as a sounding board. Lord knows my board is empty."

Julie laughed. "You're pretty funny, Molly. I'm amazed you can still laugh given what's happened to you."

"It helps not to be able to remember a bloody thing."

"I wish I could do that," Julie mused. "Sometimes I wish I could go back in time and change the past.

If only I hadn't walked in on my husband when I did."

"With another woman?"

She shook her head. "*That* I could have accepted."

"Another man?"

Julie gave an ironic smile. "Believe it or not, even *that* would have been better than what I heard and saw."

"Is your husband near here?" Molly asked.

"No."

Upon hearing the abrupt response, Molly said, "I'm sorry. I didn't mean to pry."

"You aren't prying," Julie insisted. "It's just a lot safer for us *and* for you if you know as little possible about me."

"Knowing as little as possible seems to be my forte right about now," Molly quipped.

"Sorry. It must be frustrating for you."

"Very," Molly agreed. "But in a weird way, it's also kind of...*interesting*."

"How?"

"It's as if I've had my slate wiped clean. I can be anyone or anything I want. It's sort of liberating. Except not knowing about my past also complicates things."

"Like what?"

Molly let out a slow breath. "Some woman killed herself using pills that were prescribed for me. The sheriff sounded as if he thinks I might have been some sort of accomplice in her death."

"I heard. Trust me, Molly. Unless they find some sign that you force-fed her those pills, you are not responsible for some woman's poor choice."

"Maybe. But what about the beating and the car running me down? I must have a pretty screwed-up life for those two things to have happened."

Julie sat pensively for a minute, then suggested, "Maybe you were getting your act together. A guy beat you up, you got away from him. The sheriff said you weren't from around here. I'd bet my last dollar that you were trying to get yourself out of a lousy situation."

"I didn't get very far," Molly pointed out.

"Maybe you did," Julie countered. "Remember, the driver who hit you could have just been distracted—fooling with a cell phone, looking at a map—and then fled in fear. There are endless possibilities beyond just thinking he or she intended to hurt you."

"Let's hope," Molly replied, stifling a yawn.

Julie ran her fingers through her cropped dark hair. Molly saw the beginnings of lighter roots and realized that Julie's color wasn't natural.

"I'd offer to let you rest, but Justin sent me over here with strict instructions," Julie said. "He wants you 'awake and responsive' for at least four more hours."

"Awake is a problem. Responsive seems to be on autopilot whenever he gets within ten feet of me."

Julie laughed. "He is definitely hot."

"Definitely. So what's his deal? Why is he out here in the middle of nowhere?"

"How dare you disparage Cactus Creek," Julie teased. "Population two hundred and eleven. It's actually a nice town. Nice people."

"Forget the other two-hundred and ten, what's with the doctor?"

"Justin is a good old-fashioned country doctor."

Julie's words echoed in Molly's head but it wasn't Julie's voice she heard saying them. It was a female voice, older and with a more pronounced Texas drawl.

"Molly?"

She blinked back to the present.

"Are you okay?" Julie asked, her face a palette of concern.

Molly nodded. "Just a little mental trip down a blue highway."

"Blue highway?" Julie repeated.

"On a map," Molly explained. "The smaller, off-the-beaten-path routes that few people take. They're usually colored blue on maps."

"Did you remember something?"

Molly shook her head. "Not really. I heard a voice."

"As in you remembered the sound of a person's voice? Or was it a totally psychotic experience?"

"A sixty-forty blend," Molly decided. "What you said about Justin—the country doctor thing—it was like I had heard those words before."

"It's a common expression."

"You're right, I'm sure it was just what's left of my mind playing tricks on me."

"It's good you can joke about it. I think I'd be in a full panic if I was in your shoes."

"You mean in my cast—no shoes for me for a while," Molly teased. "I was panicked. I still am on a lot of levels. I think I did denial and anger, now I'm moving into acceptance."

Julie was staring at her as if she'd just recited the Constitution verbatim.

"What?"

"That sounded...*clinical*. Maybe you're some sort of doctor or therapist."

"A battered doctor? I don't think so."

"It happens," Julie assured her. "Trust me when I tell you that education and social status can't protect you from bad things."

"Speaking from experience?"

"Firsthand," Julie acknowledged guardedly. "But back to Justin. He went to medical school back East but came home to practice. He owns this clinic, the adjoining house and property and flies his own helicopter."

"If he also wanted to eliminate hunger and prayed for world peace, could be a Playmate of the Month."

"Funny, but very close to the truth. The man definitely doesn't lack in the looks department."

Molly agreed. "Doctors should be old, white-haired and paternalistic," she commented. "Then patients wouldn't get...distracted during examinations."

"They do more than get distracted," Julie whispered, drawing her head closer. "A lot of the women around here throw themselves at Justin faster and harder than major league pitches."

"So he isn't wanting for female companionship?"

"That's the strange part," Julie softly replied. "In the time I've been here, he's had exactly one date, and then he was only gone for a short while."

"Is he gay?" Molly asked.

"Nope. Once he mentioned a fiancée."

"What happened?"

"He didn't say."

"Didn't say what?" Justin asked, walking up to the two women.

"Why you wanted Molly to stay awake," Julie lied.

Molly was impressed. Julie was quick on her feet. Yet somehow, Julie didn't impress her as someone who would lie often. What had happened to make her add those skills to repertoire?

Justin looked at Molly as he pressed his fingertips to her wrist to check her pulse.

All Molly could do was silently pray that her heart wouldn't race merely because he was touching her.

"It's a little fast," Justin commented, then replaced her arm at her side. "Because you lost consciousness, I want to keep tabs on your neurological responses for a while. I need you awake in order to do that."

I'm awake now, Molly thought, still feeling a tingle from the ghost of his touch.

"How's Thomas?" Julie asked.

Justin nodded his head. "His oxygen saturation is almost normal on fifty-percent O2."

"That's much better." Julie sounded relieved. "Can I go back with him now?"

"He's alert and waiting on you."

"I'll see you in a bit," Julie said before dashing to the other side of the room.

"Is her son really doing better?"

Justin pretended to be indignant. "Why, Ms. Parker, are you suggesting that doctors aren't always forthcoming with their patients?"

"No," Molly returned with a smile. "I was simply asking if he was doing better."

"He is. He's a tough little guy. How about you? You seem more relaxed. I hoped spending some time with Julie might help."

"It did," Molly replied in earnest. "Do you always manipulate your patients?"

"Do you always ask such direct questions?"

"I have no clue," Molly told him.

Justin shone a light in her eyes. "I wasn't manipulating you, I was…facilitating two things."

"What things?"

"Well…" He paused and slipped the penlight into his shirt pocket. "I had to draw blood from Thomas and that's more easily accomplished if Julie isn't standing over me."

"And the second thing?"

"I figured you might want someone to talk to who had an X chromosome. Women tend to open up to other women."

"You're an expert on women?"

"Not their minds," Justin admitted, then to her utter amazement, his cheeks colored slightly. "I wasn't inferring that I—"

"I know what you meant," Molly cut in, attempting to save him from himself. It was kind of nice to see him off balance for a change. However, his little gaffe just made it too easy. She couldn't let his comment pass. "Though I would expect a physician to have full and complete knowledge of the female anatomy."

"Let's say we change the subject," Justin suggested with a slight catch in his voice. "I opened the door and now I'm closing it."

"Fine, but I did enjoy seeing you blush."

He tossed her a warning glance. "I'm sure you did, but my job is to heal, not flirt."

"If that was flirting, you need some serious work."

He grinned at her. "Not when I put my mind to it."

Molly found herself fighting the urge to return the grin. She felt warm and giddy and a whole host of other inappropriate things. Didn't this guy know he didn't have to flirt? Those incredible eyes were inviting enough.

"New topic," Molly agreed as she averted her gaze

to the tips of his scuffed brown boots. "Let's negotiate bathroom privileges."

"You don't have any."

"That reply is not in the spirit of the meaning of
negotiate."

"I can get you a bedpan."

Molly fervently shook her head. "I would rather
remove my own spleen with an oyster fork than use
a bedpan."

He chuckled. The sound was deep and guttural and
far too appealing.

"Since you feel strongly, have you ever used
crutches?"

Her answer was a sidelong glance.

"Right. Okay. Mrs. Beasley should be here any
minute. I'll have her help you out."

"Thanks."

"Don't thank me yet. You haven't met her."

CHAPTER FIVE

JUSTIN SHUFFLED some of the mounds of papers on his desk, clearing away enough room to type a note about Thomas. Julie hovered nearby. She was a devoted mother. And like most mothers of sick children, she had made it her business to learn all about her baby's condition. Justin knew that parents often needed to learn about the procedures used on their children. It gave them a sense of control. Julie was now well-versed on oxygen saturation levels and could read the monitor as well as any trained professional.

Glancing over his shoulder, he took a quick look at Molly Parker. This was the first case of trauma-induced amnesia he'd seen since finishing his residency. He suspected the quick humor was part of her normal personality. He also suspected that it was her defense mechanism. He felt more than just a small measure of admiration. He'd seen far too many women broken by abuse. Molly's spirit was bruised, but not broken. Maybe she got out early.

Maybe you should get back to the job at hand, a little voice inside him chided.

"STOP SLOUCHING!" Nurse Beasley commanded.

Molly did her best to stand as straight as possible. She also swallowed a rather nasty retort. She feared the crusty nurse might pummel her with one of the crutches if she dared mouth off.

Julie wasn't helping much. Her newfound friend was snickering across the room, just loudly enough to earn her a stern yet silent reprimand from the elderly woman.

Justin had ducked out the door the instant the private duty nurse had arrived. Apparently Mrs. Beasley had been hired to watch out for Thomas. She wasn't exactly thrilled to see Molly added to her patient list.

In less than five minutes, Molly had her pegged as a retired Army nurse. It was written all over her. The nurse's uniform was white, crisp and adorned only with her nursing school pin. She wore matching white support hose and functional white orthopedic shoes. Her white hair was tucked into a tight, unflattering bun that made her head appear too small for her large, squared body. Molly guessed the only feminine thing about this woman was her name.

"Do I have to get the bedpan?" the nurse threatened.

Only if I can shove it down your throat. "No, ma'am. I'm doing the best I can. Call me a wimp but this is a little hard with a cracked rib."

"If you manipulate the crutches the way I showed you, you are in no danger of further injury to your ribs, Miss Parker."

Molly again attempted step closer to the bathroom.

For what felt like the umpteenth time, the nurse ordered, "Brace and swing."

"I'm getting it," Molly called over her shoulder. "I'm shuffling right along."

"Be cautious, Miss Parker. That doesn't mean you have to do this at a snail's pace. I have to see to the infant and you're wasting valuable time."

Molly managed to swing and hop another step closer to her goal. "Do feel free to attend baby Thomas," she said almost insistently.

"I can't, Miss Parker. Dr. Dale left strict instructions about your care—even though I was only hired to tend young Master Thomas, and general nursing duties were *not* discussed. I told the doctor when I agreed to help him out that I wasn't interested in returning to full-time patient care. I *am* retired."

"I won't tell if you don't," Molly suggested. She felt a small stream of perspiration between her shoulder blades for her well-criticized effort.

"I'm an honest person, Miss Parker."

Molly finally reached the bathroom, little thanks to the nurse. "I'm sure you're a pillar, Mrs. Beasley." She managed to maneuver herself close to the door.

"You must leave the door open," the nurse barked. "This isn't a hospital. There's no call bell in there in case you need my help. You are not a very cooperative patient. I'll include that in my notes to the doctor."

Molly met her stern green eyes. "You make notes?"

The gruff woman nodded. "I think it's imperative for medical records to accurately reflect patient care and disposition."

"Then don't forget to make a note about your disposition," Molly instructed with a saccharine smile. "Write down that you don't work and play well with others."

"Miss Parker—"

Molly closed the door and turned the latch. She completely ignored the woman's muffled rantings. The nurse finally quieted but Molly lingered after taking care of her needs.

Then she made the huge mistake of looking in the mirror as she washed her hands.

Forget that her face was unfamiliar! That wasn't nearly as shocking as its condition. Superficial scrapes and scratches marred the left side, while the right side had purplish bruises around a slightly swollen eye.

There was another bruise by her mouth, but like the one near her eye, it looked older than the scratches.

In short, she looked hideous.

Carefully, she braced herself against the countertop and gently finger-combed her tangled hair, then pulled some of the wavy strands forward in a fruitless attempt to conceal the bruises. Though it seemed pretty pointless, Molly took a paper towel from the dispenser, wet it and washed the remaining dried blood away.

What she needed was a brush, some shampoo and, failing that, a pair of scissors. A gallon of concealer might help, too.

Molly acknowledged the incessant calls from Mrs. Beasley by simply telling her she was fine, without opening the door as instructed. Instead, she tried for another thirty-five minutes to make herself more presentable, then gave up. In addition to looking like the bride of Frankenstein, she had a bit of a headache, her ribs hurt, and she was now teetering precariously on the crutches.

As unpleasant as it would be, it was time to go back out to the nurse from hell. Mrs. Beasley was probably ready to whip her with a stethoscope.

She balanced both crutches in one hand in order to unlock and open the door. One minute she had her hand on the doorknob and the next thing she knew, she was falling face first out of the room.

She gave a tiny yelp just as she felt big, strong hands grab her. The metal crutches hit the floor with a ping but she was barely conscious of the sound.

Her senses were assailed by the scent of subtle, woodsy cologne. With her palms flat against his chest, Molly could feel solid muscle beneath soft fabric. When she gathered herself together enough, she peered up into the chastising gaze of Dr. Dale.

Feeling his warm breath wash over her face had rendered her momentarily mute. All she could manage to do was stare up into those mesmerizing, thickly lashed eyes. His mouth was parted ever so slightly, though his lips were drawn into a tight, disapproving line.

One of his hands snaked around her body, gripping her at midback. In one motion, Justin hooked his other arm behind her knees and swooped her off the ground. Reflexively, Molly linked her arms around his neck as he carried her back to bed.

The action seemed effortless. There was no labor in his breathing, not even an adjustment in the way he walked. After gently placing her on the bed, he stood back, his hands resting on his hips. At that instant, he appeared rather imposing. And sexy beyond words.

"I wasn't thrilled to get an urgent page from the nurse."

Molly looked around and found Mrs. Beasley fiddling with Thomas's breathing machines. "Don't raise your voice to me. I had no choice but to page you."

"Which wouldn't have been necessary if you had behaved," Justin chided Molly.

"I was behaving," Molly scoffed. "Just not, apparently, to the liking of Nurse Ratched here."

She saw a flicker of amusement in his eyes. Still, he kept the severe expression in place. "You're restricted to bed until further notice."

"Thank you, Doctor, but I don't think so."

His face became contorted with a blend of frustration and anger. "I had to cut my rounds short because of you. Your little display of defiance caused me to miss checking on several of my patients."

Molly cringed. "Sorry," she said in a barely audible voice. "But I had no way of knowing that Nurse Beasely would bother you just because I neither wanted nor needed assistance using the bathroom."

"Yeah? Well, then what in the hell were you doing in there for nearly an hour? You suffered a head trauma, Molly. How can we monitor you if you lock yourself away like some spoiled, petulant child?"

"I was trying to clean myself up a bit," she replied in an equally loud tone. "Think of it as that 'mind-body' component of medicine. If the mind is happy, the body heals faster."

He rolled his eyes. "Did you get your M.D. watching afternoon talk shows?"

"Did you cut the classes on treating the patient as a whole person and not just the injury?" she shot back.

"You may not know your name, but you sure know enough to be incredibly infuriating!"

"I'm not infuriating," Molly insisted. "All I did was go to the bathroom and try to wash up. You and Mrs. Beasely are the ones who made a federal case out of it."

He was quiet for a minute. "We'll call this miscommunication and forget it."

"Does that get me off bed restriction?" she pressed.

He shook his head and sighed very loudly. "Molly, do you know it *is* socially acceptable to just let something drop?"

"Fine, you bring the crutches over here and I'll let the whole thing drop."

Justin rubbed his face, trying to maintain his composure. It wasn't an easy task. He was still flustered by the memory of having her in his arms. Molly was hardly the first woman he'd come across in his practice, but she was the first to conjure less-than-professional fantasies. Fearing his face might convey his thoughts, he lifted her chart and made a valiant pretext of reviewing it.

But his mind wasn't really on the results of her last neuro check. He was mired in trying to understand why he felt this sudden and intense attraction to a woman who was handling more baggage than O'Hare Airport at peak travel season.

She had lifted her arms and crossed them behind her head. Peering above the metal edge of the chart, he noted that she was staring at the ceiling. From her expression, he could tell she was still feeling confrontational. It made little sense that this woman was the victim of domestic assault. She had too much vivacity and apparently never knew when to back down.

He might have considered it possible that she'd been beaten in a mugging or a carjacking, but her X rays told him a different tale. There was evidence of several healed spiral breaks in her arms—classic signs of fractures caused by extreme twisting rather than a fall or blunt trauma. Her jaw had been broken at least once, and there was also evidence of skull fractures in her past. All that added up to repeated beatings over a prolonged period of time.

The past injuries were so prolific and the recent ones so vicious, Justin knew that whoever was responsible probably wasn't going to be satisfied until she was dead.

And none of that seemed to fit the woman he had been treating for so many hours. She had self-esteem, usually one of the first things to be extinguished by repeated abuse. She had a sense of humor and was intelligent. But most contradictory of all, she seemed to have absolutely no fear of men.

That knowledge gave him permission to continue his fantasies. He knew better than to notice her body in a non-clinical way. Knew better than to notice that she had a perfect shape. That her throat was long and graceful and fairly invited him to press his lips against her pulse points. Knew better than to wonder what it would feel like to run his palms over her flat stomach, then inch higher in order to cup one perfect, round breast.

He knew better, but his body didn't seem to care.

Luckily, he was saved from himself by the return of Alec Younger. The sheriff was a longtime friend and a welcomed diversion. At least for him. Molly didn't seem overly thrilled, though.

"Hey, Alec," Justin greeted as he replaced the chart on the hanger by the bedside.

"Justin," the sheriff returned as he removed his Stetson. "Ms. Parker."

"I'll say hello back if you tell me you've come bearing good news."

Justin couldn't read Alec's expression but he certainly picked up on Molly's unease. Without giving it much thought, he reached out and took her small hand in his. Her palm was clammy and he thought he detected the slightest of tremors.

"I have some news," Alec began, taking a notepad from his shirt pocket. Flipping it open, he read, "Molly Elizabeth Parker—maiden name Keifer."

"Maiden name?" Molly parroted with anxiety. "I'm married?"

CHAPTER SIX

"TECHNICALLY, yes," the sheriff answered, again glancing at his notes. "At least until you have your final hearing before a judge in Austin."

Justin watched as Molly's face became a canvas of pain and confusion.

"So who am I?" she asked in a subdued voice.

Alec's expression softened. "You're a waitress at a steak house in Austin, but when I called, they said you had been a no-show for work for almost a week."

"A steakhouse waitress," Molly repeated, seemingly trying on the new title.

"You've got a pretty extensive history with the Austin PD," Alec supplied.

Justin felt her squeeze his hand. He returned the gesture, hoping to give her some sense of comfort.

"I'm a criminal?"

"Nope," Alec answered quickly. "The sergeant I spoke to indicated that your house was a regular stop on their patrol routes. It seems your soon-to-be ex-husband beat you regularly."

Justin watched Molly wince. "Lovely," she said in a mere whisper.

"You left him several times over the past three

years, but he always managed to track you down.''
Alec took in a deep breath. ''You had rented an apartment, and three days ago several of your neighbors
called the cops because they heard you screaming.
But when they arrived, they found your apartment
trashed, some blood, but no signs of you or Jeb Parker. They were actually kicking around the notion of
classifying your case as a possible homicide.''

''What a mess,'' Molly breathed.

Justin found himself wishing he could spend about
ten minutes alone with this Jeb Parker person. It
would be pretty cathartic to give the guy a taste of
his own medicine. ''So what now?'' he asked Alec.

''When the PD questioned Jeb, he insisted on filing
a missing persons report. I really should call them
back and tell them we've got their missing person.''

''You can't do that!'' Justin thundered. ''We both
know that unless there's a juvenile involved, police
reports are public records. Telling the Austin police
where she is would be tantamount to sending her
sleazy husband an invitation and a map.''

Molly gripped him more tightly and gave his arm
a tug. ''Please don't let him do that. At least not until
I've had a chance to clear out of here.''

As if it were the most natural thing in the world,
Justin reached over and stroked her cheek with the
back of his hand. ''We'll figure something out, but
you aren't leaving. You need medical supervision and
rest. You can't be running all over the state of Texas,

especially when you wouldn't recognize your husband if he was wearing a sign.''

"She needs to go back to Austin," Alec said. "Her restraining order expires at the end of the week and she has to appear in court for her divorce to be final.''

"Not yet," Justin said with conviction. "I hardly think a judge will find her competent if she can't even remember her own name. Do me a favor?''

"You mean another favor? Not telling the Austin PD what I know is probably going to cost me.''

Justin sent his friend a grateful but impatient glance. "Find out who her lawyer is. Maybe something can be worked out without Molly having to risk going back to where that lowlife is probably lying in wait for her.''

"I can buy you some time," Alec agreed. "But not a lot.''

"Anything," Justin responded with gratitude.

"There's still the matter of the Pierce woman's death," Alec reminded them.

Justin scoffed. "After everything you've discovered, do you really think Molly ran off so she could help a total stranger kill herself?''

"All I know right now is the woman died of an overdose of pills prescribed to your patient.''

"C'mon, Alec. You've been in law enforcement long enough to know the desperation women feel in an abusive situation. Have you checked out Sara Pierce?''

"She had a Louisiana license. We're still waiting for information on her."

"What about on me?" Molly asked. "Do I have family? Parents? Close friends? Anyone who can help me remember?"

"Your parents are both deceased," Alec told her after another glance at his notes. "You were an only child. And as far as anyone in Austin knows, you kept to yourself. Even your neighbors at the apartment complex could only describe you by hair and eye color and height. Apparently you made a point of guarding your privacy."

"Can you blame her?" Justin asked, only then realizing he had spoken his thoughts aloud. "Obviously she didn't keep a low enough profile if Parker found her and beat her again. You did say she has a restraining order, right?"

"That is about to expire," Alec confirmed. "Instead of trying to subvert the system, why don't I file a report here, then send it to the Austin PD and they can pick Parker up on the RO violation?"

"But then he'd know where I am, right?" Molly asked in a panic.

Justin held her hand against his chest. The tremor had evolved into a continuous shaking. "Alec may have a point. It would be a way to get your husband into a jail cell."

"You swear, right?" Molly asked, her eyes wide and doelike.

"Judges don't like it when folks ignore their orders,'' Alec answered. ''Between an angry judge and some pretty pissed cops, I think your husband is a candidate for a long stretch as a guest of the city.''

He felt Molly relax somewhat.

''I wouldn't have to go back to Austin?''

''I'll write a medical report for Alec to include.'' Justin winked at her and added, ''In my humble medical opinion, you are in no condition to travel.''

''It also keeps me off the crap list of a reciprocal law enforcement agency.'' Alec seemed relieved.

''So how will this work, exactly?'' Molly asked.

''First I call the sergeant in Austin and fill him in,'' Alec explained. ''Then I write my report, attach Justin's medical findings and send it through the channels. I'll also shoot a copy to your attorney. I'm sure the PD can get me that information off the restraining order.''

''What about J-Jeb?'' Molly stammered.

''The cops will pick him up and take him before the judge. Armed with my report and Justin's medical findings about your recent beating, I'm sure they'll toss him in jail on contempt.''

''And he'll have to stay there?'' Molly asked.

Alec nodded. ''Thanks to sensitivity training, most judges are pretty harsh on batterers who ignore their orders.''

''Then what?'' Justin asked. ''Can she go back to Austin for her divorce hearing?''

He felt a shiver emanate from the whole of Molly's small frame.

"I imagine," Alec replied. "I would guess that Parker has some legal right to be brought from jail for the actual hearing, but the bailiffs can keep him shackled if her attorney makes a request."

"What do I do until he's caught?"

"I'll take care of you," Justin said, then, noting the shocked look on Alec's face, he amended his remark. "I mean, I have to take care of your injuries. You can stay here."

"In a clinic?"

Justin sighed. "It's the best I have to offer."

"I didn't mean to sound ungrateful," she insisted. "But this is a place for sick people and I'm really not sick."

"We'll work something out," Justin promised her. "I'll see Alec outside. Be right back."

The two of them stepped out into the cool, night. Justin wished it were colder, as in a cold shower.

"What are you doing, my friend?" Alec asked pointedly.

"Seeing to the best interests of my patient," Justin replied with as much propriety as he could muster.

Alec cupped his hands to light a cigarette. He blew out a long stream of bluish smoke, then said, "I think it's more like you're interested in seeing your patient."

"I care about everyone I treat," Justin defended lamely.

"Which is why I'll tell you for the hundredth time you really should give those things up."

"Taken under advisement," was Alec's rote reply. "We've known each other since we were kids, Justin. Which means I know when you're lusting."

"Don't be an ass."

"Me?" Alec said with a hearty laugh. "I'm not the one getting all hot and bothered over a woman who is A, under your care, B, in a world of hurt and trouble, and C, married."

"*Technically* married. Your words."

"You'd be more than just a *technical* idiot to get involved with her," Alec stated bluntly. "It took her a long time to leave her husband. It will probably take her twice as long to get her life together. You'd be nothing but a crutch for a woman on the rebound. You really want that kind of trouble?"

"I can't figure out what I want," Justin admitted.

Alec snorted and took another pull on his cigarette. "Well, then maybe the two of you have something in common. You don't know what you want and she doesn't know who she is. You can build a relationship based on mutual confusion."

"Tell me again why we're friends?" Justin asked.

"I've got your number, Doc. Even when you're thinking like an ass."

"You don't know what I'm thinking."

"Yeah, right. I know you too well. You're as transparent as a hooker's bra. You held her hand. You stroked her cheek. Classic signs."

"Of compassion."

"You were trying to score points," Alec accused

good-naturedly. "Doing all those things you see in chick flicks."

"I was just trying to keep her calm."

"So that's why you put her hand on your chest? Who are you kidding, Doc?"

"Is there a point to this male-bonding conversation?" Justin asked, slightly irritated.

"Always. I know that stuff with Tina threw you for a loop. But believe me, taking on the Parker woman's problems isn't the way to go."

"I haven't taken on anything."

"All you need is some armor and a trusty steed and you'd look just like her knight protector. Not a smart move when neither one of you knows anything about her."

"I didn't hear you say you found anything bad in her past."

"Didn't you hear the part about the abusive husband? *Husband* being the important part. And let's not forget the dead woman in Pinto or the fact that she has amnesia. Personally, I would think any one of those things would be sufficient to warn off any sane man."

"I haven't done anything, Alec. Lighten up."

"But you want to," Alec remarked knowingly. "As your friend, I'm just trying to tell you that you're headed down a dangerous path. Personally, I think you'd be better off with Julie."

Justin let that pass. He'd only told Alec the bare minimum about Julie—his friend didn't know she was hiding from her husband, too. Keeping his word to Julie required as much. Besides, he had always thought of Julie in a benign, sisterly way. Nothing like the intense interest he'd felt when he had first laid eyes on Molly.

"Stella said you and Julie were locked in deep conversation last night at the Blue Moon," Alec repeated.

"To paraphrase you, *conversation* being the important part."

"I'm just trying to watch out for you, Doc. Especially when I see your thinking coming from somewhere south of the border."

"Go catch a criminal," Justin said. "I've got things to do."

Alec started walking toward his marked car. Over his shoulder, he called, "And I'll bet one of those things is Molly Parker. Mistake, Doc. Big mistake!"

CHAPTER SEVEN

SHE WAS DREAMING. No, not exactly. It was more like a nightmare, only she was awake. Kind of.

The room was all shadows and quiet save for the rhythmic hissing of the baby's oxygen pump.

She blinked, trying to capture some lucidity in her jumbled thoughts. At first, it was as if she were viewing a series of flash cards. Eventually, the pace of the mental images slowed and melded into coherent memory.

Her first clear recollection was of being a bride. A happy, beaming bride, walking down an unadorned aisle to an attractive, muscular man positioned next to the cleric. She remembered feeling lucky, excited—giddy. Above all, she remembered that the man about to become her husband was Hank Allen Pierce.

"Oh, God," she prayed, closing her eyes against a sudden flood of warm tears.

Sara sobbed in near silence as the pieces of her pathetic history fell back into place. She remembered a marriage that had been great for two weeks. Then the patterns of beatings and apologies had begun. Hank Allen's cold, icy blue eyes seemed to be tattooed on her soul. No matter how she tried to redirect her thoughts, Sara could still feel the fear and horror she had experienced at his hands.

She remembered almost every ugly detail of her life. Mostly, she remembered that Hank Allen was going to kill her.

"What's wrong?"

Sara opened her eyes and found Julie's disquieted face at her bedside. Sara tried a weak smile as she attempted to pull herself together. "B-bad dream," she lied.

"Thomas is sleeping comfortably," Julie said. "I'll sit with you for a little bit."

Sara couldn't seem to stop the flow of tears. Or stem the tide of panic. There were some things— some pieces—that didn't quite fit.

"How long have I been here?" she asked.

The question caused immediate concern for her companion.

"You've been here a day and a half," Julie explained slowly. "You were in an accident, Molly."

Molly. Sara's brain kicked into high gear. They all thought she was Molly Parker. Molly Parker whose husband was going to be arrested and put in an Austin jail to keep her safe. The Molly who had seen no light at the end of the tunnel of horrors and had given up. The Molly who had let her abusive husband win. Most important, the Molly Parker who had no reason to fear Hank Allen.

"Molly?" Julie repeated with some urgency.

Sara brushed the tears away. So everyone thought she was Molly. That was exactly what she had hoped for when she had taken the younger woman's identification at the shelter. Right?

"You don't look good," Julie said. "I think I should page Justin."

Sara didn't respond, she was way too deep into her own thoughts. Nothing had changed, really. She still needed a new identity and basically she had one. Recalling the two visits from the sheriff, she also knew that Molly Parker didn't have any children or parents grieving her loss. Best of all, Molly Parker's abuser was on his way to jail. She was safe. She could start over. Being Molly Parker would be easier and healthier than going back to being Sara Pierce.

Julie reappeared, still looking somewhat frantic.

"I'm fine," Sara said, believing it for the most part.

"You weirded out there for a minute. Justin should be here in a flash."

"You shouldn't have disturbed him," Sara insisted. "The nightmare is over." *In more ways than you know.*

Julie cocked her head to one side. "There's something different about you."

Sara feigned innocence. "I don't know what you're talking about. I'm fine, really."

Julie shook her head and persisted. "You've lost that confused look. In fact—" Julie pulled a small cord and a light flickered on overhead "—you look almost relieved. I didn't think nightmares were supposed to do that.''

Sara shrugged. ''I'm relieved I'm not having a nightmare anymore.''

''That isn't it,'' Julie guessed. She scrutinized Sara for several seconds before asking, ''Have you remembered something?''

Sara shook her head. ''No, I'm as blank as ever.''

''What's the problem?'' Justin demanded when he appeared.

It was obvious that he had been sleeping. His thick dark hair was disheveled and he had incorrectly buttoned his shirt. Sara knew she shouldn't have noticed the dark curls of chest hair visible above his rumpled shirt. She even knew she shouldn't be wondering if that thick mat of hair tapered into a neat *V* before disappearing into the waistband of his jeans. Jeans, she now noted, that he had zipped, but not buttoned.

He was exuding a little too much attractive masculinity for her overloaded senses. That had to be why she was aware of the faint stubble covering his chin. And equally aware of her own strange desire to reach up and stroke the beginnings of his beard.

''I had a bad dream and Julie freaked.''

Her comment earned her a silent reprimand from Julie.

''Your cheeks are tear streaked,'' Justin said.

Does he have any idea how incredibly sexy his voice is when it's raspy from recent sleep? Do I have any idea why I'm thinking such outrageous things?

Sara sank back on the pillow, hoping distance might keep her mind in check.

It didn't help when he reached down and ever so gently used his knuckles to dry the tracks of her tears. That simple action, coupled with the intensity of his dark eyes, made her heart flutter.

"Do you remember your dream?"

Hearing his slow, sensual drawl nearly made her forget to breathe. "Not really."

When Justin pulled his hand away, she stifled the urge to grab it and hold it against her cheek. Lusting after a handsome doctor wasn't part of her plan.

"I'm going to give you something to help you relax," Justin said.

"No!" she exclaimed. "I don't need anything. Besides, I hate taking medications."

His dark brows drew together questioningly. "You know that. Or you're guessing?"

I'm blowing it! "I—I just meant that I hate the *idea* of taking anything. Under the circumstances, I'd like to remain as lucid as possible."

Somewhat grudgingly, he accepted her explanation at face value.

Justin asked Julie to give them some space, and then he turned to Sara and asked, "Need to talk?"

"About what?"

He sat on the stool and raked one hand through his already mussed hair. "Anything. Alec provided a lot of details earlier. They weren't all pleasant."

"But he provided a solution, too," she reminded him. "Jeb Parker will be arrested, and as soon as you give me the okay, I'll be on my way."

His expression blended confusion and something akin to disapproval. "You left a step out."

"What step?"

"Going to Austin to get your divorce?"

I don't think Sara Pierce can divorce Jeb Parker. "I'll tend to the legal formalities eventually."

Justin fairly exploded at her. "Are you telling me that you're not going to go through with your divorce? Didn't you hear Alec?"

"Of course," she insisted. "But I'd just like to know more about Molly—I mean, *me*—before I make any decisions."

Justin let out a slow string of epithets. "You have an opportunity to get a fresh start right now, Molly. Divorce the guy and be free of him so he can't hurt you ever again."

Actually, I've already done that, Sara thought with amused disgust. *My divorce decree wasn't a very good shield.* "I just want to take it one step at a time. First, I need to know that Jeb Parker is in jail."

Justin met and held her gaze. "Are you still in love with him?"

"Trust me, I'm not in love with him. In fact, I'm very sure I was never in love with him."

"How can you know that?"

"Instinct."

MOLLY. MOLLY. MOLLY. She repeated the name over and over in her mind, willing herself to think of it as her own. It had been two days since she had remembered the horrible truth about herself. Even though she had agonized about her deceit, self-preservation won out.

"You're supposed to be in bed," Justin said as he entered the clinic and tossed the battered leather backpack he used as a combination medical bag-briefcase onto the top of the desk where she had taken up residence.

"I'm going a little stir-crazy," she admitted, greeting his smile with one of her own. For a scant second, their eyes met. She could only describe the feeling as a small explosion in the pit of her stomach. Justin Dale had the uncanny ability to heighten all her senses just by existing.

"You're violating patient privileges," he chastised as he came alongside her and began to check the labels on the folders she had divided into five neat piles.

The faint scent of soap clung to his large frame and she silently begged her conscience not to notice. Again. It was becoming something of a ritual. Every time he got within a few feet of her, Sara—*Molly*, she mentally corrected—suffered a hormonal surge that would have put any adolescent to shame.

"You have no organizational skills," Sara told him.

"Guilty," he agreed easily as he hoisted himself up onto the edge of the desk. "I've never been great at all the forms and letters that go with the territory."

There is nothing wrong with your form, her traitorous mind concluded. Sara averted her eyes, afraid some of her lecherous thoughts might be evident in her expression. Getting a grip on her feelings—shallow as they were—for the handsome doctor were part of her new plan.

"That's why I'm setting up an interface and configuring a single-use station for you."

"Huh?" Justin was peering down at her, and his eyes seemed to glaze over at her explanation.

Taking in a slow breath, Sara reached out and adjusted the computer screen so that Justin could see it more clearly. "You have all the tools right here, you just haven't been using them effectively."

"That seems to be the story of my life," he commented rather wryly.

Was that some sort of double entendre? Sara wondered. She could *only* wonder, since she should know better than to trust her own instincts when it came to men. Was it arrogance that made her wonder if Justin was interested in her, or was it simply that she was misreading the intent of his kindness? It didn't matter. As soon as she was mobile enough to travel, she knew she would probably never cross paths with the gorgeous doctor again. *Focus,* she told herself sternly.

"I've noticed that you use a palm device or a laptop to make your patient notes and do your dictation," she began in the best professional voice she could muster.

"The palm thing was a gift from a passing computer rep. I lanced a boil for him."

"Lovely," Sara muttered. "Well, it has complete interface capabilities with your desktop computer."

He stroked his chin. "Complete interface, huh? Should I be worried about unplanned pregnancies?"

Sara laughed at his humor. "No, you should be worried about unplanned lack of payment. You see, you have filing deadlines for insurance reimbursement. I've already found seven instances where you would have received partial payment for services except that you didn't bother to get the forms to the insurance companies in a timely fashion."

"The patient got treatment, that's what matters."

Sara sighed in frustration. "Treating people is obviously your forte. But I don't think it's a violation of the Hippocratic Oath for you to receive just compensation for your work."

He leaned back on one arm. Mere inches separated his muscled chest from her face, and Sara found it a little more than just distracting. It was annoying. Or thrilling. Or maybe both.

"Contrary to popular belief, I'm not in this for the money. I never was."

"I can see that from these records."

He chuckled. It was a deep, soothing sound that seemed to reverberate through every cell in her body.

"So you're going to save me from myself?"

"Maybe," she suggested, growing a little annoyed at his obvious dismissal of her abilities.

"Thanks, but I don't have time to learn the inner workings of medical software."

"Someone should. Don't you have an office manager?"

"Nope."

"What about Mrs. Beasley?" Sara suggested. "She certainly strikes me as the kind of woman who thinks organization is next to godliness."

"Once a Marine, always a Marine," Justin quipped. "And if I were you, I wouldn't even think about suggesting she take on extra duties."

"She'd be perfect at it."

"She's suspicious of computers," Justin explained. "Thinks they're all some sort of porthole into the private lives of average citizens. And she resents change. If it isn't broken, she doesn't fix it."

Undeterred, Sara said, "But I can set up a really simple program. You can use your palm organizer when you see a patient, then upload the information into the system. Then let the system generate insurance forms, tell you when you need to follow up, that sort of thing. I can even arrange to have it order medical tests based on your diagnosis."

Justin was now giving her his full attention. "Show me."

Sara took the top folder and scanned the chart. "I haven't written all the fields into the program yet, but if this kid came back, you could—" she paused as her fingers flew across the keyboard, making entries "—tell the computer what you know, list the symptoms and…'' The computer's hard drive whirred for a second, then the letters *BE* flashed red against a blue screen. A test order form popped up, preaddressed to the hospital in Fort Worth. ''See, it almost instantly tells you what to do next.''

Justin took the chart from her hand, then alternated between reading the chart and looking at the screen.

''*BE,* huh?''

''Sure,'' Sara said, trying to hide her sense of pride at her accomplishment. ''Barium enema, right?''

''Just so I get it, all I would do is click that button and the computer would order *that* test for *this* patient?''

Sara smiled unabashedly. ''Exactly.''

''I doubt five-year-old Jeffrey Grimes would appreciate having a test that would give him a radioactive colon.''

''But Mrs. Beasley wrote *BE* right here in the chart,'' Sara said, grabbing it from Justin.

''It means *broken extremity.* Jeffrey climbed a tree and tried to fly. Made it about two feet before he hit a lower branch.''

Sara pursed her lips. ''Okay, so there's a few glitches to be worked out.''

''Glad to hear you decided that before I turned Jeffrey's intestines into night-lights.''

Using her good leg, Sara swiveled in the chair and tilted her head up to meet his eyes. ''I guess I'm overstepping my bounds. I was just bored and thought I might be able to help.''

The look he gave her made Sara's spine liquid. There were soft lines around his eyes, and the simple way he cocked his head to one side gave him an air of strength and confidence that she found incredibly appealing. But it wasn't just his physical attractiveness that seemed to reel her in. It was the underlying kindness, the compassion, the notion that he was simply a good, decent man.

That had to account for her unexplainable and uncontrollable response. She'd never known a man like Justin. Never thought men like him existed except in movies or books. But here he was, in the flesh. And she wasn't quite sure how to handle it.

Justin had been handling it fine. At least that's what he'd been telling himself. But now, looking into her big brown eyes, he knew he wasn't handling anything. This woman was like a magnet, and he was pulled to her every time he walked through the door of his clinic.

He'd been hiding behind the fact that she was his patient. That way he was safe. But her physical injuries no longer required his medical attention. The bruises and abrasions were healing and the cast would come off in a few weeks. It was her emotional injuries that should have acted like a brick wall. The amnesia, though he was sure it was only temporary, was still present and technically required monitoring. Her past made her vulnerable.

There were so many ethical reasons why he should quell his feelings before they got the better of him.

Unfortunately, his gut and his brain seemed to be taking divergent paths. Molly intrigued him. And this latest talent of hers only fueled that interest. She was smart, computer savvy and seemed to know her way around a doctor's office. He respected the fact that she was so capable. It was admirable that a woman who had suffered so much in her twenty-four years was still able to function. No, it was more than just functioning. That was the strange part of all this. He would never disparage waitressing, but Molly didn't seem like a typical waitress. Her computer prowess alone cast doubt on that fact. Since she obviously had these skills, why was she working as a waitress?

Right then, right there, he couldn't see past the golden starbursts that lent an exotic air to her brown eyes. He no longer saw the faint discoloration around her mouth. Instead his gazed fixed on her slightly parted lips. He stared for a long time. He felt a teenagelike inability to control himself.

He shouldn't kiss her. Hell, he shouldn't even be *thinking* about kissing her. But there she was, with her dainty chin lifted ever so slightly. He could hear the faint raspiness of her uneven breaths spilling over her lips.

Suddenly the spark between them became palpable. Before he could even think, his palm was resting against her cheek and his head was dipping lower.

He stopped just shy of her parted lips. His fingers slid softly over her cheekbone until just the tips were lost in the thick mane of silky hair that framed her upturned face. The look in her eyes was wild, primal, and not the least bit apprehensive. For a millisecond, he wished she had given him some signal, some warning to his brain that would have been more effective than his obviously absent conscience.

Her breath was warm against his mouth. She smelled of floral shampoo and desire. It was a combination that was about to get him into serious trouble. He was losing himself and his good judgment, and worst of all, he didn't care.

Until the phone rang.

They jerked apart. Sara was actually shaking. And it wasn't all the result of adrenaline caused by the sudden blast from the telephone. Even as Justin ripped the receiver off its cradle, Sara was already dissecting her behavior.

She couldn't look at him. And she wasn't too thrilled with the mental picture of herself. Kissing Justin Dale, as appealing as that thought was, was not part of her new plan.

"It's for you."

Sara blinked. "For me?"

He nodded and handed her the phone. For a scant second, their fingers brushed and their eyes locked. She had expected to see remorse or disgust or even an expression of regret. What she saw was unmasked, unbridled passion, and she knew immediately that she felt the same.

"H-hello?"

"This is Trevor Pope. I'm trying to reach Molly Parker."

The male voice was unfamiliar. Sara's desire quickly gave way to a small wave of panic. Justin was still at her side, she was stuck.

"Speaking."

"That you, honey? You don't sound like yourself."

Tapping the phone, she said, "Bad connection, I think. Whom did you say were calling?"

She heard a hearty, beefy laugh. "Geez, Molly, they got you takin' diction courses down there? Well, I guess it won't hurt when we get y'all in front of a judge."

"I'm a little confused."

"Yeah, right! That fine sheriff said you was having a few...difficulties with your memory. How is my girl feelin', by the way? I can't tell you how furious I was when I heard what that no-account husband of yours did this time."

"Thank you."

"Don't thank me yet. We got us a problem."

"Problem?"

"You sure you're all right, honey? I swear you don't sound like yourself."

"Fine," Sara insisted, though she spoke as softly as she could without alerting Justin.

"I got all the papers from those kind folks in Cactus Creek. I can't tell you how relieved Wanda and I were when we heard you were okay. I thought for sure Jeb had done you in this time. I talked to Wanda and we agreed that you could come and stay with us until your divorce hearing.''

"No!"

"Why, Molly, honey, I'm only trying to look out for you. I'm working with the police to try to find Jeb as we speak. And I'm more than just your lawyer, I'm your friend. Wanda, too. We aim to help you through this.''

Lawyer? I can't meet with this man. He'll know I'm not the real Molly in a heartbeat. "I'm fine here," she insisted. "I want to stay in Cactus Creek for a while. If I need anything, I'll call.''

"Call nothing! I need you here, Molly. I can get the restraining order renewed without you, but you've got to appear in court to finalize your divorce.''

"I'm not ready for court," she said. Sara felt Justin's eyes bore through her like lasers. "I need some time.''

"Molly, honey?''

"I'll call you.''

She hung up the phone and wondered what she would say to Justin. As it turned out, she didn't need to say a thing. He was gone.

Alone in the clinic, Sara wished Julie and the nurse hadn't had to take the baby to Fort Worth for a consultation with a specialist. She was glad Thomas was well enough for the brief outing, but she sure could have used a friend.

"And tell her what?'' Sara grumbled.

"Hey, there!"

Sara almost tumbled out of the chair when the postal worker bounced into the clinic balancing a few boxes and some letters in her arms.

"Doc out?"

Sara nodded.

The woman deposited the items on the desk and offered Sara a cheerful smile. "You tell that handsome man I said hey, okay?"

"Will do," Sara promised.

"Good to see you up and about," she fairly chirped as she opened a glass canister on the edge of the desk and helped herself to a lollipop.

"Good to be up," Sara agreed, adjusting the cotton blouse that Julie had donated. Julie's generosity had also provided her with jeans she was able to wear after cutting a slit in the left pant leg to accommodate the cast.

"I guess you'll be leaving soon."

Sara almost laughed aloud. She knew small town interrogation couched in friendly conversation when she heard it. "Soon."

"Glad you're feeling better."

"Thanks."

The letter carrier turned to leave, then called back, "That one on the top is for you. Found it out on the front step."

She reached up and took the plain white envelope from the stack. Molly Parker was typed in bold capital letters. Probably from the sheriff. But why would he leave it outside?

Sara slipped her finger beneath the flap and broke the seal. She removed the single piece of paper. When she read the two words on the sheet, her blood froze in her veins.

CHAPTER EIGHT

"WHAT DO YOU think you're doing?" Justin fairly thundered, gripping her upper arm. The move was half intended to steady her and half to gain her attention.

"I have to go. Now."

"Go where?"

She gaped up at him. Her eyes mirrored the sheer panic he had heard in her tremulous voice.

"He knows I'm here. You saw the note. I'm not safe here."

"Alec is on his way," Justin told her, hoping to calm her a bit. It didn't work.

She didn't pull free of his grasp. Molly needed him to keep her balance since she was unsteady because of the cast.

"Let's talk about this," he suggested.

She rolled her eyes. "What is there to talk about? There's a man out there who knows where I am who has very clearly made his intentions known."

Justin thought about the note. The image of the black block letters spelling out "You're Dead" was emblazoned on his brain. "You can't just hobble off."

"Yeah? Watch me."

Molly half turned and literally crumpled into his arms. Justin lifted her and carried her to the nearby exam table. "You shouldn't be putting weight on that ankle."

She simply glared at him, her rosy lips pulled into a taut line.

"Okay." Justin raked his hands through his hair, then rested them, palms down, on either side of her. "I agree that you need to be someplace safe. How about the Harrisons?"

"No!"

"Won't you even consider it?"

"I'm better off if I go someplace new, someplace he won't know to look for me."

Frustration and unabashed anger surged through him. "That doesn't seem to have worked so far."

"No kidding."

"You need to take the necessary steps to get him behind bars and then out of your life."

"I think I've tried that, Doctor. At least that's what everyone keeps telling me. Until an hour ago I thought he was being arrested."

"Until the phone rang, I thought you were going to divorce him," Justin countered, feeling his own anger and frustration.

"Divorcing him is the least of my worries," she said.

It struck him as odd that she was so casual about the idea. It seemed to him that she would have wanted to take every legal step possible to get the man out of her life. Unless she still had feelings for him. That was troubling. Justin could have lied to himself. Pretend that his annoyance about her ambivalence was based solely on his experience with battered women. Intellectually, he knew that she could be in a pattern common in abusive relationships. She could be thinking that she could repair the relationship with her husband.

But that didn't seem to fit. Molly's tone was derisive whenever she said her husband's name. And that brief almost-kiss. It just wasn't adding up. Molly acted more like a woman who had healed than one who was still mired in abuse. He felt like he was looking at all the pieces to a complex puzzle, but incapable of putting them together.

She had earned his respect and admiration. The very things that he found so attractive were also responsible for his confusion. She gave every indication that she wanted to move on with her life, so why stall on the divorce?

"It should be a priority," Justin said. He realized he must have yelled the words since they were echoing off the walls of the clinic.

"I don't understand why you're giving me grief about this," Molly complained. "Just give me one of those orthopedic boot things so I can walk and I'll be on my way."

"Well, I don't understand a lot of things about you."

"What's to understand?" she retorted in a tone that matched his in force and volume. "I've got a lunatic who wants me dead and I don't want to be dead. See? Simple."

"There's more here, Molly." He thought he saw a flicker of something in her eyes, but it quickly vanished.

"Look, thanks for everything, but I need to go before something terrible happens."

"I'll arrange for Alec to protect you."

She scoffed. "I'm sure you've seen enough battered women to know that there is no such thing as protection. For heaven's sake, Justin, he was close enough to leave that note."

Justin scratched his chin. "So why didn't he just come inside?"

"What?"

"Why didn't he come in and attack you?"

"Sorry to have disappointed you," she grumbled.

He grasped her upper arms and gently shook her until she met his gaze. "Something isn't right here. He had an opportunity to get to you and instead he just left a note. Why?"

"Maybe he saw someone or someone saw him," Molly suggested. "Or maybe he's a cruel psychotic who enjoys playing games. Like some animal that toys with its prey before losing interest and killing it."

Justin changed his grip to slowly massage her tense

shoulders. "Or maybe he doesn't really want to kill you. If that's the case, you should stand up to him."

"Before or after he breaks another rib?"

Sucking in a breath, Justin tried to put his jumbled thoughts into some cohesive order. "Of course I didn't mean I think you should put yourself in danger. I'm just trying to look at the possibilities here."

"I have the very real possibility of being dead soon. Is that clear enough for you, Doctor?"

"It's even more of a possibility if you leave. How far do you think you can get with a broken ankle? Even if you go someplace else, that cast will make it hard for you to blend in."

"Why am I arguing with you?" she groaned. "This isn't your problem."

"I'm making it my problem."

"Why?"

He didn't answer her. He couldn't. He didn't know the answer.

Alec saved him by arriving then. If his scowl was any indication, his friend wasn't in the best of moods.

"Everybody okay?" he asked.

Justin nodded. "Glad it wasn't an emergency. You certainly took your time."

His friend shot him a warning look. "Sorry. You said there was no sign of Parker and I had to take a call. You got a problem with that?"

Justin was a little taken aback by his friend's un-characteristic challenge. Lifting his hands in mock surrender, he said, "Sorry I snapped at you, Alec. Can we get down to business?"

Alec's expression softened but Justin could see he was troubled.

"Believe me, I should have dodged the call and come here."

"Was it about Jeb Parker?" Molly asked.

Justin hated the tentative way Molly said her spouse's name. Or maybe he just hated her spouse. No, he definitely hated him.

"Roundabout way," Alec supplied. "I was talking to the ex of the woman who died in Pinto."

"He's here?"

Justin heard the fear in Molly's voice and grasped her hand. He wanted to kick Alec. Molly didn't need to know that Cactus Creek was being overrun with abusive husbands just now.

"No, he's right where he should be. But that's not important now. Where's the note?"

Justin grabbed the offensive piece of paper and attempted to hand it to Alec.

"You two the only ones who touched it?" he asked, pulling a clear bag from his shirt pocket.

"The mail woman," Molly supplied.

"I can have the state crime lab check for prints, but something tells me ol' Jeb is a little too smart for that."

"Yeah," Justin grumbled. "It takes real brains to threaten a defenseless woman." Molly was still trembling. He curbed his instinctive reaction, the one urging him to pull her into his embrace.

"But you did find Mr. Pierce, right?" Molly asked.

"Look," Alec began calmly. "If you're thinking Hank Allen Pierce is going to come after you because he was told his ex-wife's death is still under investigation, don't worry."

"You're sure?" Molly pressed.

Alec nodded. "I played phone tag with the guy for two days. Apparently he owns a string of gyms and doesn't keep regular hours. He finally called me from his cell phone and, well, let's just say that he didn't have a very compassionate suggestion for what we should do with his ex-wife's body when the coroner is finished."

"Sounds like a great guy," Justin drawled. "I'm going to assume that in light of the note, you can't still think that Molly had any involvement in the Pierce woman's overdose."

"Look, I'll tell you what I know so far." Alec pulled a small notepad from his breast pocket. "The tox screen on Mrs. Pierce indicated that she died from acute barbiturate poisoning. Her stomach still contained some undigested pills."

"That means suicide," Justin stated.

Alec met his gaze. "It would seem that Mrs. Pierce did take her own life. But there are still a couple of problems."

"What problems?" Molly demanded.

Justin allowed his hand to slip down and cover one

of hers. She clutched his hand in return. The fear emanating from her small frame was unmistakable.

"The autopsy indicated that she had been taking Xanax on a regular basis," Alex said.

"What's that?" Molly asked.

"An antianxiety drug," Justin explained. "She was most likely taking it for acute panic attacks."

"That's what the coroner said," Alec agreed. "But that's one of the problems in this case."

Justin sighed. "Alec, it's completely reasonable that she'd be treated with that particular drug. It's commonly prescribed."

"So I've been told. Problem is, Mrs. Pierce's doctor and her ex both swear she wasn't taking it."

Justin thought for a moment, then suggested, "From what you've told me, I doubt Mrs. Pierce was confiding in her abusive ex-husband. Maybe she didn't get the script from her regular doctor. She could have been seeing a therapist."

"I'm checking on that," Alec told him. "The second problem is a little stickier."

"In what way?"

"The Harrisons are pretty shook up. They said they ask all their new arrivals if they're carrying any drugs. They have a strict policy about drugs at their place and they're insisting that you lied to them during your intake interview."

"They didn't ask me about drugs!"

Justin peered down at her, confused by her outburst. "You remember going to the Harrisons?"

Her eyelashes fluttered, then shrouded her eyes. "No, but—but I'm sure I wouldn't have lied."

"Let's hope not," Alec warned. "The Harrisons get some state and federal funding for their shelter. If you're charged with assisting a suicide, they're off the hook for not following procedure."

Sara let out a slow breath. "I would *not* have helped that girl kill herself." *What do I do now?* she wondered.

"I'm not in any hurry to arrest you. But the Harrisons have some pretty influential friends. It would help if you could remember," Alec prodded.

Oh, I remember. I remember every time Hank Allen beat me. Now he thinks I'm dead and I'm safe. I can't go backward. I won't. Unless I'm arrested. Then I won't have a choice.

Sara met his eyes. "Yes, it would, but I can't." She slid her hand free of Justin's. Somehow it didn't seem right to accept his comfort and compassion when she was lying like a rug. It was time to go on the offensive. "Why wasn't Jeb Parker arrested? You told me it would be easy to put him behind bars."

Alec had the decency to look contrite. "Apparently Jeb's cousin's neighbor's daughter is file clerk for the Austin PD."

"Great!" Sara groaned.

"She did get fired, but not before she told Jeb you were here in Cactus Creek."

Sara shoved Justin out of the way, then teetered precariously at the side of the bed. "I have to get out of here." If Jeb found her, Sara knew, her plans would be ruined.

"Molly!" Justin spoke her name like a command. "Get out of panic mode and let the three of us work this out."

Tilting her head, she gazed up into his chocolate eyes. "Why should I panic?" she retorted hotly. "Just because a well-intentioned couple wants me arrested to protect their behinds and a violent psychopath knows where I am? You're right. I can't imagine why I'm not serene."

"Hang on," Alec interjected.

Grudgingly, Sara turned her attention to the sheriff. "Hang on for what? What if Jeb comes here? I'm putting Justin and Julie and the baby in jeopardy."

"You forgot nurse Beasley," Justin said with a lame half smile.

"She could probably take him," Sara quipped. "But okay, her too. I don't have the right to put other people in danger."

"You're right," Justin agreed. "Maybe the clinic isn't the best place for you, but that doesn't mean you have to leave."

"I can put her in protective custody," Alec suggested.

Sara laughed without humor. "Wonderful! I get to go to jail while Jeb Parker roams free."

"I have an alternative," Justin said.

"A nice big rock for me to hide under?"

"Actually, I was thinking of a quaint guesthouse."

"Hey, Doc…"

Sara heard the caution in Alec's tone. Justin appeared to ignore his friend's unspoken warning.

"It beats jail," Justin defended. "And I doubt her husband would go looking for her at the guesthouse."

Alec's face clearly conveyed his disapproval. "You're asking for trouble."

Justin met her eyes and said, "There's a small guesthouse on my property. You could stay there long enough to heal."

"It's too isolated," Alec argued.

"It's got an alarm system," Justin said. "At night you can make sure one of your deputies swings by every hour or so."

"What about during the day?" Alec asked.

"She can stick close to me."

"She'd be safer in jail," Alec countered firmly. "This is a police matter, Doc."

"What will it be?" Justin asked her. "Your call."

Sara weighed the options. She didn't relish the idea of going to jail. But she also wasn't too thrilled with the notion of being alone at night. Then again, she was an expert on abusive men. And Jeb Parker had already shown her part of his hand. He'd left the note outside. Just like her ex-husband, Jeb was too big a coward to attack his wife in front of others. Sara knew she had one other thing working in her favor. If Jeb ever did find her, he wouldn't beat her. He had nothing against Sara Pierce.

CHAPTER NINE

JUSTIN WAS TRYING, pretty much in vain, to keep his mind on reviewing the stack of charts Molly had given him. She had set about computerizing his practice and they were down to the older files. She claimed his handwriting was something akin to Sanskrit, so she had assigned him the task of deciphering his own notes.

They were working like a well-oiled machine. It was as if Molly could anticipate his next thought. Which was pretty unsettling, considering the fact that she still hadn't regained the individual memories of her personality.

He didn't much mind; he liked the person she was now. He peeked at her above the folder. Her face was a mask of concentration. The intervening weeks had healed her facial injuries, revealing her stunning beauty. She was certainly pretty enough to turn any man's head, but that wasn't what Justin found so attractive. Her mind and her humor were incredibly appealing. The fact she was so attractively packaged was a bonus.

Molly was more than just efficient. She was exceptional and had computer skills that he could only dream of. She was also incredibly good with his patients, even the ones feigning illness in order to check her out. At least once a day one of the town residents would drop in. He knew from Stella at the Blue Moon that gossip was raging through the town. Many of his neighbors were speculating on the true nature of his relationship with Molly.

He felt himself frown. He didn't have a relationship with Molly. At least not the kind he could define.

"You need to write a treatment plan for Mr. Gilmore," Molly said without looking up.

"I did."

Lifting her head, she met his eyes. It was like being touched.

"Not according to the insurance company."

"The man has diabetes. He's on insulin."

He listened as Molly's fingers tapped the computer keys.

"You've seen him three times in the last month," Molly said. "Don't you think you should send him to Fort Worth for managed wound care? That ulcer on his foot isn't healing."

"Thank you for that second opinion, Doctor," Justin teased. He smiled when he saw her cheeks color. "For your information, Mr. Gilmore refuses to go to Fort Worth."

"Sorry," she muttered.

He shrugged and leaned back in his chair. "Don't be sorry. Your suggestion was right on target. Not bad for a steak house waitress."

She cast him a sidelong look. "You shouldn't criticize those who serve."

"It wasn't a criticism. It was a compliment." His remark only seemed to deepen her blush. "Maybe you should think about college."

She averted her eyes.

"I'm serious," he continued. "You're bright, capable and you've got a great eye for detail. You would breeze through."

"Uh-huh," she mumbled.

Standing, Justin walked around to her side of the desk and placed his hands on her shoulders. She smelled of floral shampoo. He felt the slight tensing of her small frame. "I'm serious, Molly. You should start thinking about your future."

The slight tension became palpable. "Hard to have a future when you don't have a past."

"You don't need one," Justin asserted. "Not to go to college, at least."

"No, you just need time and money. Time I've got, money is a problem. Let me work, please," she said, brushing at his hands.

Justin hadn't thought about her financial status until that moment. He had given Julie money to buy Molly a few clothes and personal items, but that was when she'd first moved to the guesthouse. "You've been working hard. I'm more than happy to pay you for what you've done."

She shook her head. "This is to defray the costs of your bill," she insisted. "At some point in time, when

I'm off earning a living, I'll pay you for everything you've done.''

"That isn't necessary," Justin said, feeling slightly saddened that she felt obligated to him.

"Sure it is."

"You've helped me, Molly." And that was true. Justin hadn't realized how much he'd grown to enjoy her company. How he looked forward to seeing her every morning. How much he loved seeing her smile or listening to the sound of her voice. He had gotten comfortable with her. No, *comfortable* wasn't the right word.

He liked his life. Loved his work. He felt fulfilled and had achieved his goals. But Molly had brought something into his life he hadn't known he was missing. The idea that she would vanish from his life filled him with an overwhelming sense of loneliness.

He was being incredibly selfish, he chided himself. Molly needed to heal and build her own life. The last thing she needed was a relationship.

So why is that the only thing I want?

"WELCOME," Sara greeted Julie after unbolting the three shiny new dead bolts that had recently been installed on the guesthouse door and punching the alarm code.

"Thought you could use some company."

Sara could have hugged her. Justin had been away from the clinic all day so Sara had remained at the guesthouse. "Company and-or therapy," she joked.

"These nights alone have made me a little squirrelly. Not to mention being cooped up all of today."

Julie walked into the large, rectangular room that served as living space, dining area and kitchen. She placed a picnic basket in the center of the round, claw-foot oak table Sara had spent hours dusting and polishing over the previous three weeks.

"I brought us dinner."

Sara smelled yeast rolls and dill and her mouth began to water. Limping over, she helped Julie unpack the basket.

"Grilled salmon with dill, new potatoes, fresh salad," Sara listed, feeling almost giddy that she wouldn't have to eat yet another frozen meal.

"And an unpretentious Chablis." Julie smiled as she grabbed the bottle and opener. "Justin said a little wine wouldn't hurt."

"Where is Justin?" Sara asked, careful to keep the disappointment out of her voice. Although she saw him during the day, she looked forward to his nightly visit to check on her.

Julie eyed her suspiciously. "And here I thought you'd be happy to see me."

"I am!" Sara insisted. "I guess he's just become a habit."

"An attractive habit," Julie agreed with a conspiratorial grin. "The truth is, he had to go check on old Mr. Hawkins. He's still complaining about back pain."

"Ten bucks says it's a kidney stone."

Julie pulled the cork from the bottle and was now staring at Sara.

"What?"

Pursing her lips, Julie held her gaze for another second, then started to pour wine into glasses she had brought along. "You seem to have an awful lot of medical knowledge for a waitress. I've seen the way you've been coding and organizing Justin's files. You can correctly spell medical terms I can't even pronounce and I've been at the clinic for longer than you."

Sara was careful to avert her eyes. "I must just be a good speller. Who's baby Thomas with tonight?"

Julie's face beamed. "Nurse Beasley agreed to stay with him so I could come for a visit. He still has to have someone with him who can handle a crisis. But it's looking better. He's almost off oxygen and Justin seems really pleased with his progress."

"You've got to be relieved. I can't imagine what it must feel like to have a sick baby."

"Believe me, you don't want to know." Julie handed Sara a glass of wine. "Do you ever think about having kids?" Julie chuckled. "Sorry, I guess that's a stupid question."

Scooting out one chair, Sara took a sip of her wine as she sat. "Actually, these nights I've had plenty of time to think. And I would like kids—but only with the right man."

"I've got to warm this stuff," Julie said. She carried the dishes to the oven and opened the door.

"We've got to find you something more to do," she exclaimed. "This oven looks brand-new. Come to think of it, the whole place looks freshly scrubbed."

"I have run out of things to spit and polish," she admitted. "I've never been good at relaxation."

Julie's look again became suspicious. "Never?"

"Never as in not in the past few weeks." Sara wasn't convinced she had covered her slip-up. "How long does that have to reheat?"

"If you need to talk, I'm a good listener," Julie said, ignoring Sara's lame attempt to change the subject. "I know what it's like to feel alone and isolated."

Sara smiled. "I appreciate the offer, but I really don't have any reason to bend your ear."

Julie looked as if she wanted to press the issue, but thankfully, she opted not to. Joining Sara at the table, she took a drink and grinned. "This is the first time since Thomas was born that I've had a girls' night out."

"Do you really consider dinner here at Fort Guesthouse a night out?"

Julie laughed. "Sure. And it's all thanks to Mrs. Beasley."

"The nurse from hell," Sara injected.

"I'll agree that she isn't the most personable woman, but she's great with Thomas. That's all that matters."

"It is a little weird that she's so sweet with the baby and so nasty to everyone else."

"She'd probably never admit it, but I think she regrets the fact that she never had children."

"Darwin would applaud that fact. She eliminated 'surly' from the gene pool."

"Now who's being nasty?"

"Guilty," Sara sighed. The wine was relaxing and it was good to have someone to talk to. "You're lucky to have your son."

"No argument from me. Thomas is the joy of my life."

Sara traced the rim of the glass with her fingertip. "A life with joy in it. Obviously a concept I never mastered."

"I see alcohol brings out the self-pity in you."

"One part self-pity, an equal dose of self-loathing," Sara mused.

Julie frowned. "You can't possibly think you're in any way responsible for your husband's actions."

"I didn't get into this mess by accident," Sara said.

"You're no more to blame for your husband being a loser than I am for my husband being what he is."

"What is he?"

"Dangerous," Julie responded solemnly.

"As bad as Jeb Parker?"

"Maybe. Maybe worse in some ways."

"What can be worse than a man who is so cruel that suicide becomes an option?"

Julie's expression instantly registered concern. "You're not thinking of doing anything stupid, are you?"

"No," Sara assured her. "I was just thinking about Sara Pierce. I think I can understand why she killed herself."

"Well, I can't," Julie insisted. "One thing I've learned these last months is that we have the power to change our lives."

Sara laughed, though the sound was devoid of humor. "Don't you think this conversation is a little on the ironic side since both of us are currently in hiding?"

Shrugging, Julie said, "Point taken. But I intend on building a new life for myself and Thomas."

Sara raised her wineglass to Julie's. "Here's to new lives."

Luckily for Sara, the conversation lightened as the evening progressed. She and Julie discussed everything from clothes to current events. After their meal, Julie built a fire in the fireplace to ward off the chill.

The guesthouse was quaint and very masculine. Like the man who owned it, Sara thought privately. The pine floors were unvarnished. The roof trusses and beams were exposed and the walls were paneled in knotty pine.

The furniture was also rustic. The chair and sofa were crafted out of branches that had been bent and molded into shape. The cushions were overstuffed and soft, and covered in a bold Native American print. On the walls were paintings of cowboys and Indians from the Old West.

The bedroom was comfortable but sparsely furnished. That wasn't much of a problem since she only had the half-dozen outfits Julie had bought or donated to her. Sara guessed the bed was old—at least the iron looked old, especially with the handmade, bottle-cap quilt covering mattress.

The bathroom had all the modern conveniences, but it was the color scheme that was dated. The wallpaper featured patterned earth tones that had been popular three decades earlier. She probably would have retired the olive-green tub and basin, but it wasn't her call.

Taking one of the cushions from the back of the sofa, Sara settled in near the fire with her third glass of wine.

She sipped it as Julie fell into the chair with a deep sigh.

"Want me to make some coffee?" Julie asked.

"And ruin a perfectly good feeling of euphoria? No way."

"I don't think Justin will approve of me getting you drunk."

"First, I'm not drunk, and second, why would he care?"

Julie rolled her eyes. "Probably for the same reason he's trying so hard to maintain a professional distance."

Sara hated herself for asking, but she couldn't help it. "Which is?"

"He's interested in you."

Sara's heartbeat caught for a split second. "As a patient."

"As a woman," Julie corrected. "But he's too decent to do anything about it."

"I'm indecent?" Sara queried.

"No. But I'm sure he thinks it's inappropriate to make an advance to a married woman."

"But I'm not—" Sara swallowed the rest of the sentence. "I'm not *really* married."

"I don't think Justin is the kind of man who would split that hair. Nor would he take advantage of you when you can't remember your life. Which you can't, right?"

"Right." Sara closed her eyes briefly. She would laugh if the situation weren't so pathetic.

"Are you sure I can't make some coffee before I go?"

Shaking her head, Sara said no and thanked Julie for the dinner and the friendship.

"Lock up," Julie reminded her as she took out the car keys and headed for the door. "Maybe I can stop by tomorrow afternoon. Justin and I are taking Thomas to Fort Worth for a lung scan in the morning."

"I'd like that, but don't put pressure on yourself. Your baby needs you. That's a long trip."

"Not by air. Justin's flying us there himself."

"He's a pilot?" Sara asked, surprised.

Julie paused with the door ajar. "I told you that the first day, but I guess it didn't register. He's a man of many talents."

"I'm sure," Sara demurred.

"You aren't convinced after everything he's done for you?" Julie asked, genuinely shocked.

Sara traced the edge of a floor plank with the toe-plate of her cast. "I'm sure he's wonderful. But you can never *really* know another person."

Alone again. After washing the dishes, Sara stoked the fire, watching the flames dance in protest before flickering up into the chimney.

"What are you doing, Molly?" she mumbled. "Or rather, Sara." Actually, she had begun to think of herself as Molly. At least she was comfortable with the name.

Easing herself down to the floor, she stared at the flames. If Julie hadn't already figured out that she wasn't what she seemed, it was only a matter of time.

"Until what?" Sara whispered to herself. "I need money and transportation," she decided. Too bad Molly's identity hadn't come with some cash.

Everyone had been so nice to her, she felt guilty about her deception. As she lay in front of the fire, she actually wondered if she dared to tell Julie the truth. In the end, she decided it wouldn't be a smart move. Julie and Justin were friends and she doubted Julie would allow herself to become complicit in her scam.

But what were the alternatives? Tell the sheriff? Alec had spent the last three weeks paying his staff overtime to protect her from a dead woman's husband. Somehow she doubted he'd be too thrilled if he found out she was an imposter.

The biggest threat was Hank Allen. As much as she hated deceiving her new friends, it didn't come close to her fear of another beating. She had to stick to her plan for a while longer. Once the cast was off, she'd leave and no one would be the wiser.

She would miss Julie and Justin.

"Justin." His name was a whisper on her lips. Obviously the fates weren't finished toying with her yet. Only she would be unlucky enough to land in some small town with a gorgeous doctor.

Gorgeous seemed insufficient to describe him.

"A drop-dead-handsome doctor," she whispered.

No, more than that.

"A drop-dead-handsome doctor who is also a *pilot*."

Still not enough.

"A *nice*-drop-dead-handsome doctor-pilot."

Not there yet.

"A nice-drop-dead-handsome doctor-pilot *who has the hots for me*."

Sara turned and screamed into the pillow. It was so surreal. It had taken her almost two years after her divorce to accept an invitation for a cup of coffee from a guy in her statistics class. What a disaster that had been. He was nice and she had enjoyed herself after a while, but he never called her for a second date. Not that she could blame him. The poor guy had cupped her face for an innocent kiss and she'd countered by kneeing him.

She'd gotten a little better since then. But now that

she was on the subject, she reminded herself that she hadn't allowed herself to be alone with a man in years. She always met her dates in public places. Except for Justin.

His image easily came to her mind. Touching her fingers to her lips, she wondered—not for the first time—what it would feel like to be kissed by him.

She imagined that with him it would be a process more than just an action. He'd probably start by stroking her cheek. He'd done it a time or two and she liked the contrast of his gentle touch and his strong hands. She knew she would be mesmerized by his eyes. They were so intense and penetrating that it was impossible not to get lost in them.

She could see the two of them in her mind's eye, standing close by the fire. She imagined her palms flattened against the molded muscles of his chest. His breath would be warm against her upturned face. Anticipation would virtually buckle her knees. But the kiss would come at his pace. And his pace would be deliberate. His fingers would splay across her cheeks as his thumbs moved teasingly toward her slightly parted lips. Her breath would catch in her throat. Her heart would be racing in her ears. Still, he would hover just out of reach, leaving her wanting, stirring long-dormant desires.

The promise of his anticipated kiss would darken his eyes, but still, he would linger. The pad of his thumb would brush across her lower lip like a whisper. She would clutch fistfuls of his shirt to keep from falling. Her body would arch against his. Primal need would suffocate reason.

Slowly, he would increase the pressure and rhythm of his thumb against her lip. Passion would lock their gazes as he touched her. A gasp would spill from her mouth. Then a groan when his fingers entwined in her hair.

Justin would dip his head another fraction, stopping just short of giving her what she wanted with utter desperation. She would moisten her lips with her tongue. His gaze would drop to her mouth. Her arms would snake around his neck, pulling him to her. Letting her feel the level of his arousal against her belly.

No longer able to control herself, she would get up on tiptoe while pulling his mouth to hers. She would taste him. Her body would be on fire and her mind…

"I don't have a mind!" She sat bolt upright. Rubbing her eyes, she tried to banish her thoughts. Unfortunately her fantasy had been a little too vivid. Her heart was actually racing and her hand trembled. She struggled to stand. "I've been alone too long."

Behind her, a male voice said, "You aren't alone now."

CHAPTER TEN

"OH, MY GOD!"

"No, only Justin," he responded with a very sexy, crooked grin.

"You scared me into the next millennium!" she yelped.

"Sorry. The door wasn't bolted. You should be thinking about safety."

I definitely wasn't thinking about safety. He looked utterly manly standing there in his jeans and beige cotton shirt, his tie askew. His thick hair was ruffled, probably because of his habit of running his fingers through it. There were faint lines at the corners of his eyes due to fatigue, and her first instinct was to go over and put her hand on his cheek.

Okay, it probably wasn't instinct. More like the residual longings courtesy of her vivid fantasy. She felt her face warm with color. Her upbringing in a Catholic orphanage was at serious odds with her recent guilty pleasure.

"Are you okay?"

"Couldn't be better," she said, forcing a smile. "Julie came by, we had dinner."

It took him only two strides to reach the table. He

lifted the empty wine bottle and cocked his head at her. "Obviously dinner wasn't all you two had."

"Don't worry, we didn't have any boys over and we only made three crank phone calls."

"Cute, Molly. Phone calls are one of the reasons I stopped by."

"I haven't touched the phone," she swore. "I don't need to, I don't have anyone to call."

"Trevor Pope?"

It took her a minute to remember that he was Molly's divorce lawyer. "Right. Sorry. I forgot."

There was an awkward silence, made worse by the fact that Justin's eyes never left hers. There was an unspoken challenge in his look. And something else. Something akin to disappointment.

"Is there some reason you're dragging your heels about getting a divorce?"

"Heel," she corrected with a sly grin. "Currently I have only one heel at my disposal."

His expression grew serious as he lowered his large body into a chair, then motioned for her to do the same. He rubbed his face with his hands, then used those intense eyes like a weapon. "I debated a long time whether to come over here or not."

"Why?"

"Because this is complicated."

"*This* being…?"

"You. You're complicated."

Sara let out a breath. "I know this has been an

imposition on you. If you'll loan me a little money, I can be on the next bus out of here."

He half snorted, half laughed. "With all the work you've put in computerizing my clinic, I should have been paying you a salary from the start."

"You gave me room and board. By the way, *board* is an apt description for those nasty frozen meals you stocked in the freezer."

He grudgingly smiled. "How is it that you manage to find humor in everything?"

"You know what they say, laugh so you don't cry."

"That remark is illustrative of my point." He drew in a deep breath and let it out slowly. "I've done a little research into amnesia."

"If you're going to do a paper on me for one of those boring medical journals you leave lying around the clinic, would you mind waiting until Jeb Parker is in jail?"

"I'd prefer to see Jeb Parker in hell."

"I'm sure he'll get there eventually," Sara agreed easily.

"I've found cases similar to yours. Complete functionality but total erasure of personal history. All of the cases cite emotional and-or psychological reasons for the memory disruption."

"Did you come here to tell me you're having me committed?"

"Of the two of us, I'm the better candidate for involuntary commitment."

"You seem completely functional to me." Sara grinned as she imitated the tone and cadence of his voice.

"I'm not."

Her jovial mood ebbed as she took in his serious expression. "Don't look so forlorn, Doctor. I appreciate everything you've done for me. Don't feel guilty because you're too polite to come right out and ask me to leave. I've already offered to go and I meant it."

"You're too smart to be this dense." Irritation punctuated each word.

Sara experienced a fleeting feeling of fear at the hint of anger in his voice. She had come a long way, but she still found it hard not to be afraid. She was choked by a lump in her throat.

"Why do you look like I just kicked your dog?"

"Wh-why are you angry at me?"

He shook his head. "I'm not angry, Molly. Well, maybe I am, but at myself, not at you."

"You've been wonderful to me. You should feel good about yourself for being so kind and generous with me. You've selflessly gone above and beyond the call of duty."

"My motives aren't completely selfless. Since the only further medical treatment you need is to have your cast removed, I can refer you to an orthopod for follow-up. Which then means I am not your doctor and I definitely don't consider you a duty."

Trying to lighten his mood, she asked, "Are you

resigning as my doctor? I'd prefer not to be turfed to another doc, assuming I get a vote here."

"I don't want your vote." He held her gaze. "I want you."

Sara went completely still.

He looked as if he would give anything to take those words back. "I didn't mean to say it like that. I meant that I wanted to get to know you."

"In the biblical sense?"

He smiled at her. "You're never at a loss for words, are you?"

"Guess not."

"And the answer to your question is probably."

"Only probably?" She hoped her disappointment had remained a private thing.

He scooted the chair closer to hers, reached out, and caught her hands in his. "I'm a man, Molly. Whether I want to or not, carnal thoughts do enter my mind when I think of you."

She gave him an outrageous wink. "So you're admitting that the cast is a turn-on?"

Justin felt himself squeeze her hands when what he really wanted to do was kiss her senseless. "Can we have a conversation here, please?" Her big eyes were full of apprehension in spite of the playfulness in her tone. "Let me start over," he suggested, regrouping his thoughts. It wasn't easy for him to stay focused when he could feel the silky softness of her skin. Thick, wavy hair framed her face and fell about her shoulders. Yet again he imagined that mane of hair splayed against his pillow. Imagined running his fingers through it.

"So start," she prompted.

Justin blinked, clearing his head. "I've been less than forthcoming with you."

"About?"

"My interest goes beyond the professional."

"You have lust in your heart?"

"This would be easier without your commentary."

"Sorry."

"I know the last thing you probably want or need is a man to further complicate your...situation."

"I believe a man *is* the complication in my situation."

He shot her a warning look and she closed her mouth. "Maybe this was a bad idea."

"I think you can put admitting that you'd like to have sex with me in the negative column, if you're critiquing."

Justin felt like an awkward, gangly teenager trying to have a coherent conversation with the prom queen. "Done, but regardless, I promise you that I am fully capable of controlling my libido. Believe it or not, I'm much more interested in getting to know you. Which is the crux of my problem."

"Why?"

He found himself gaping at her. "To state the obvious, getting to know you is a little on the impossible side when you don't know yourself." He again rallied his thoughts. "I like you, Molly. Not just because you're beautiful. If that was the only basis for my attraction, I wouldn't be here right now.''

''Thanks, I think.''

''I'm just trying to be honest with you. Honesty is important to me.'' She pulled her hands out of his and he figured that wasn't a good sign. ''Before I say this the wrong way *again,* let me give it another try. When you first came into the clinic, I was impressed by your looks.''

''So I guess what they say is true, you *do* have to suffer to be lovely.''

''Luckily for you, blood doesn't bother me. Then you came around and I discovered the impossible.''

''Amnesia?''

''No, that your beauty was only surpassed by your brains. You're an incredible person. One I'd like to get to know.''

''Which is why you've been the perfect professional with me?''

''Of course,'' he answered. ''I know you need time to rediscover yourself. I'm also reasonably sure that once you get your memory back, the last thing you'll want for a while is another man in your life. As a physician, I know you should take your time and rebuild your life. Unfortunately, I'm a physician who also happens to be human.''

''So why are you telling me this?''

Justin blew out a breath and leaned back in his chair. ''Confession is good for the soul.''

''So whose soul benefited from your confession?''

"Mine," he admitted. "I probably shouldn't have said anything, but I can't stand pretending I don't have these feelings whenever I'm around you. I promised myself a long time ago that I would always be honest with my relationships and expect honesty in return."

"That has the ring of a eulogy for a failed marriage."

He offered a wan smile. "Engagement, actually. Turned out she didn't love me."

"That could cause a failure."

"In all fairness, I think Tina loved her vision of life with me."

"Which was?"

"The right house in the right neighborhood with the right friends at the right country club."

"I take it Cactus Creek doesn't have a country club?"

"According to Tina, Cactus Creek doesn't have anything. I brought her here once and she likened it to an Outward Bound experience."

"Prefers a city, huh?"

"I don't think she can be more than ten minutes from the closest pedicure. Anyway, when I told her I was coming back here to practice after my residency at Hopkins, she canceled the wedding."

"At least you were spared a messy divorce."

"Which brings up another obstacle to our getting to know one another."

"What?"

He blinked again, not sure he had heard such an obtuse question fall from her mouth. "Divorce. Specifically yours? I'm really not comfortable with the fact that you're married."

"It's not like I'm married with a capital *M*," she argued.

"Then why are you dodging your attorney?"

"I'm not dodging him," she insisted.

She began to twist a lock of hair around one delicate, tapered finger.

"Molly?"

"I don't like Mr. Pope. I was thinking of finding a new attorney."

He scoffed in disbelief. "You don't like the attorney? A man whom you have spoken with one time for under five minutes since you've been here?"

"Not really. No."

"Do you have to like him to finalize your divorce?"

"I think I should be comfortable with him. Divorces can get ugly."

"Not yours, Alec checked. You and your husband don't have a single asset to divide. There is no property and no kids. Your grounds of cruelty are well documented by the Austin police. All you have to do is show up in court and ask the judge to dissolve your marriage."

"What do I tell the judge?" she retorted with anger. "I swear everything in these papers is true, I just can't remember any of it?"

"Mr. Pope says it isn't a problem. The judge is aware of your condition and is willing to accept testimony and affidavits from earlier court dates when you got restraining orders."

"I'm not doing anything until Jeb Parker is in jail."

"Everyone in Austin seems to believe that your husband will show up to contest the divorce even if it means getting thrown in jail."

"What will stop him from getting to me *before* he gets thrown into jail?"

"I'll go with you," he told her. "I'll fly you up there, go to court with you and fly you back. I'll stay with you the whole time."

She shook her head. "I can't do that."

"You *can* do it. Why *won't* you?"

"I'm scared. And I don't like being pressured."

"I wasn't trying to do that."

"Yes," she breathed, "you were. And you're right, this is too complicated. And also for the record, since we're being totally honest with one another, I'm attracted to you, too. But since I can't trust my feelings, there's no place to take this."

"Do you think you're still in love with your husband?"

Her laugh came out bathed in sadness. "I'm sure I don't love Jeb Parker. I'm just not sure I know how to think in terms of a future."

"I understand," Justin said, rising to his feet.

"Wait!" Molly fairly cried.

He froze, half-standing. When she looked at him with those pleading eyes, it was impossible to resist. The intelligent side of his brain knew the best move would be to leave and try to forget he'd ever started this inane conversation. Unfortunately, the sweet smell of floral soap had pretty much obliterated his IQ.

She was still twisting her hair, a nervous tick he'd noticed before. Justin just didn't know if that was good or bad. He guessed he was about to find out.

"Why does getting to know one another have prerequisites?"

He rubbed the shadow of his beard. "Because I have two rules about women."

The playful glint returned to her eyes. "Only two?"

"Two *preliminary* rules," he clarified. "No virgins and no married women."

"Julie is married and you're her friend."

"There's a difference. I don't dream about Julie." He secretly liked the fact that his direct answer seemed to knock her slightly off balance.

"Does it have to be all or nothing?" she asked in that husky voice that had cost him many hours of sleep.

"What are you suggesting?"

"There's no reason that we can't get to know one another. Why not see what—if anything—happens, and worry about the future then? Can you give me one good reason why we can't do that?"

"Absolutely." He stood and went to her. Getting down on one knee, he reached out and brushed a lock of hair away from her eyes. With deliberate gentleness, he allowed the pad of his forefinger to trace the outline of her cheek. He heard the little catch in her breath.

Mere inches separated their faces. Justin took his time, studying each delicate feature in turn. His fingers inched lower, to the pulse point on her throat. He didn't need his medical degree to know that his touch was affecting her. It was plainly visible in her eyes. The golden starbursts around her pupils seemed to explode with passion. He moved his fingers under her chin and lifted her face just a fraction. When her tongue flicked out to moisten her lower lip, he wasn't sure he could maintain control.

Her mouth was open ever so slightly. Her lips looked soft, pliant and inviting. Unable to stop himself, he touched the tip of one finger to her lips. He traced the outline of her mouth, then met her gaze.

Somewhere in the recess of his mind, he knew he shouldn't be doing this. But he was ignoring the recesses. He was ignoring everything in the world save for the feel of her flushed skin, her smoldering eyes and her uneven breathing.

All he needed to do was dip his head a few inches and he could taste her. His conscience and common sense decided to take a joint vacation at that instant, so he indulged himself without reservation.

He would pay later, but right here and right now,

all he wanted was Molly. More accurately, the want had turned to need.

It took all his self-restraint to keep from dragging her off that chair and onto his lap. He didn't back off, but when he spoke, he barely recognized the sound of his own voice. "*This* is the reason, Molly."

"It isn't a very good one," she whispered back as her arms came up and she grasped his head, pulling him to her.

Somewhere in the last few minutes, Sara had stopped caring about everything but this. The feel of his mouth on hers. The expert way he choreographed the kiss. The scent of his cologne and the raw passion were just too powerful a combination.

She hadn't felt like this in a long time. No, she amended when she felt his fingers in her hair. She had *never* felt like this. So alive. Justin's passion didn't frighten her. In fact, she found his steely control arousing in an odd way. It was as if he'd tossed out a challenge. One she was all too ready to accept.

He must have been reading her mind because he deepened the kiss into something much more sensual and intense. She dropped her palms to his chest and was stunned at the rapid, erratic beat of his heart. Stunned because it mirrored her own. She felt blood surge through her body, spreading the electric feel of his touch through her system. Desire built in the pit of her stomach.

She touched him everywhere she could reach. His broad shoulders, his powerful arms. She was memorizing his torso with her hands. Testing, molding and caressing as she explored.

When her fingertips grazed his waistband, Sara heard and felt him groan. She felt empowered. She felt in control. Control was a heady new experience for her.

She took her time, but eventually, she laced her fingers behind his neck. It wasn't physically possible, but she wanted him closer. She wanted more. She wanted him.

CHAPTER ELEVEN

HE QUICKLY ended the kiss. He was equally expedient at untangling their arms, standing and taking a step back. Her body was tingling with unrealized passion and her mind was in a state of total confusion.

When she peered up at him, his face was a grim mixture of guilt and lingering desire. He took several deep breaths before speaking. What he said shocked her brain out of its fog.

"I'm sorry."

"S-sorry?" she parroted. How on earth could he be sorry for making her feel alive for the first time in her life? "For what?"

"Breaking the rules."

Frustrated, Sara blew a breath toward her forehead. "Your rules, not mine. And for the record, it's a stupid rule. You can't possibly think of me as married, can you?"

He raked his fingers through his hair. "I don't have to think. It's a fact."

"It's a...legal technicality at best," she argued. "I don't think you'll burn in hell because we shared a kiss. Which was, if you're interested, mind-altering."

At least that produced a smile, grudging though it

was. "You truly are never at a loss for words, are you, Molly?"

"It's a gift," she mused.

"Like your gift for medical matters?"

Sara dropped her gaze. "What do you mean?"

"For one thing, you used the word *turfed* when I suggested finding you another doctor."

"Isn't that what docs say when they hand patients off?"

"Yes, but I've never said it to you and it's normally only used in hospitals between the medical staff. Never in front of patients."

She made a production out of crossing her arms. "Well, I must have heard it someplace. It could have been a game-show question for all I know."

"What about Mr. Hawkins?" he queried.

"The nice old guy with the back pain? Is it kidney stones?"

"Forget for a minute that you were eavesdropping while I was doing his history. What made you pull back the curtain and ask if he ate a lot of ice cream and drank a lot of tea?"

Any lingering passion had long been doused by a gush of panic. What if she came right out and told him the truth? She played the scene in her head.

I knew to ask that, Justin, because I worked in a hospital for two years while I was earning a degree in hospital administration. I know that the combination of tea and ice cream often causes calcium stones to form. I know all this because I'm really Sara

Pierce. And I've known I was Sara Pierce since a day after I met you.

In her mind, Justin's reaction was something akin to shock, followed by a long lecture on honesty. After that, he would walk away from her and never look back. She knew she didn't want that. She wanted to enjoy whatever time they had together before she left. As soon as Jeb Parker was behind bars, she would set out on a new life. One that didn't include being afraid.

Or being with Justin.

Maintaining the charade long enough to heal and get away was the only way she could save her life. At best, Justin could only be a footnote in that life.

"I—I must have read about it in one of your journals. Or maybe I knew someone who had the same thing in my previous life. I was only trying to help and you're making me feel like I did something wrong."

When she peered up through her lashes, Sara felt a blend of guilt and relief. Justin looked positively contrite.

"You're right," he said easily. The corner of his mouth curved into a slow grin. "I don't know where I was going with that. I suppose that kiss was mind-altering for me, too."

"Glad to hear it." Which was true. An understatement, but true. "Does that mean we can do it again?"

She watched as he waged a private war within. His eyes were signaling a definite yes, but his body language hinted that an altogether different response was forthcoming.

"As strange as this is going to sound, I can't forget that you're legally married, even though you seem to be able to."

"We're talking about getting to know one another, Justin. My marital status isn't relevant to that."

He chuckled. "Do you really think we can spend any amount of time together and stay platonic?"

She smiled up at him. "Why don't we worry about that if and when it becomes an issue?"

"It's already an issue for me," he admitted. "I was thinking about a lot more than kissing just now."

She pretended to be shocked. "Something else crossed your mind? Do tell!"

His head cocked to one side and he shot her a sexy, if cautionary, look. "I'm sure you get my drift, Molly."

She started to stand when he held up his hand and stopped her. "Stay there."

"Why? I need to tend the fire."

"You can do that after I leave. I've used my entire store of willpower tonight, so I don't want you coming close."

Again Sara felt that spike of control. Odd, but knowing she had a kind of mastery over him was a new and exciting feeling. It was like she'd been given a magical power. One she wanted to test. "Afraid I'll seduce you, huh?"

"A little," he admitted, his eyes smoldering more

than the embers in the fireplace. "I'm struggling with a principle here, Molly. Want to cut me some slack?"

"Sure. Let's negotiate."

He let out an impatient breath. "What is it with you and negotiation? Can't you simply cooperate?"

"Not as much fun," she answered. "If I promise not to attempt to seduce you, can I talk you into a furlough?"

"You're safe here."

"I'm going nuts here! C'mon, Justin. All I want to do is spend a couple of hours at the clinic tomorrow while you're in Fort Worth. I missed going today and I want to add a few things to your software program."

"No. The deal is you stay here when I have to be away."

She shook a chiding finger at him. "That is not the spirit of negotiating, Justin. I'm just asking for a couple of hours of credit for time served."

"Have you forgotten the note?"

She shivered. "Of course not, but I've also noticed that it's been three weeks and there hasn't been a single sighting of Jeb Parker."

"That's probably because I rented motel rooms in several towns in your name."

"You what?"

"Alec and I decided it would be a good idea to give Parker some false leads to chase. With the help of some of his contacts in other jurisdictions, we created a trail for Parker to follow so he would think you left Cactus Creek right after he made contact with that message.''

"And you didn't bother telling me?''

"We weren't sure it would work and I didn't want to get your hopes up.''

"I can't believe you kept me a virtual prisoner knowing full well that Jeb Parker was off on a pre-arranged wild-goose chase.''

"That's the problem,'' Justin said, his voice tinged with anger. "So far he hasn't shown up at any of the motels, so we don't know if he took the bait.''

"How do you know he hasn't shown up?''

"All seven of the motels are being watched.''

Her head began to swim. "Who told you to turn this into some major league manhunt?''

"You did,'' he answered in clipped syllables. "You said you wanted him in jail.''

"Jail first, hell second,'' she answered, remembering the lifeless body of the real Molly Parker. "How many people have you involved in this?''

"A few dozen. Mostly law enforcement friends of Alec's.''

In her mind she saw a long indictment. Filing a false police report. Obstruction of justice. Interfering with a police investigation. The hole she had dug was suddenly a canyon. She had to get out before she got trapped at the bottom.

TO SAY SHE HAD a sleepless night was a lot like saying the *Titanic* had taken on a little water. By the time the sun painted the eastern sky a brilliant palette of pinks and oranges, she had a revised plan.

Her hideout in Cactus Creek had taken on a life of its own. Too many people were involved. Cast or no cast, it was time for her to move on.

As she poured herself a third cup of coffee, Sara knew she had a major obstacle to overcome. No transportation.

Then the light dawned. "No *physical* transportation, but that doesn't keep me off the information superhighway."

Justin had given her a laptop to use at the guesthouse. It had a modem. She had a phone line. Now all she needed was some luck.

It took her a while to find the right site, but eventually she came across the archives of the *Johnson County Ledger*. Its claim to fame was being one of the oldest weekly papers in the county. Her fingers flew over the keyboard until she found the obituary section for the same year in which she was born. She didn't have any luck. She had to go back another two years before she found what she needed.

She read from the screen, "Emily Louise Ross. Infant daughter of Grayson and Melinda Ross. Died just shy of her first birthday." Sadness filled her as she carefully copied the information onto a pad of paper. She thought of how sick baby Thomas had been, but didn't dare allow herself to imagine the kind of pain Julie would feel if she had lost her son. Especially since he wasn't completely out of the woods. His lungs were still vulnerable to any opportunistic bacteria or virus.

"Stop being maudlin," she warned herself as she went back to the browser and started pulling up the official forms she would need to print, complete and mail in order to assume this new identity.

Then she hit a snag. In order to procure a duplicate birth certificate, she would need a check or money order. She had neither. Absently, she drew her lower lip between her teeth as she ran possibilities through her mind. Inspired, she went into the bedroom and retrieved Molly's purse. Dumping the contents on the bed, she picked up the wallet and began going through it until she found what she was looking for.

Molly's ATM card.

"Let's see if Molly has any money," she said as she returned to the computer. Finding the bank's site was pretty easy. She had the account number in front of her but she was denied access on a password block.

"Think!" she commanded. Most people used letters or numbers that they could remember easily. She tried using Molly's middle name, then her maiden name, then her birthdate, and even her Social Security number. Nothing. She stared down at the driver's license in her hand, willing it to point her in the right direction. Nothing jumped out at her.

"It would be ironic if you used your wedding anniversary," she told the photograph. "I don't know when you got married."

Searching for a marriage license would be like

looking for a needle in a stack of needles. She didn't even know in what state Molly and Jeb had married. That information was probably in the divorce papers, but she knew calling Trevor Pope, Esquire, was not an option. He seemed to know the real Molly well enough to tell that Sara was an imposter by voice alone. Maybe as a last-ditch effort she'd contact him. But for now, she tried to think of a back door into the bank records.

"Back door, backward," she said in something of a free-association. "Success."

Molly had simply reversed the numbers in her birthdate as her password. A few seconds later, the computer's hard drive whirred and up popped account information.

Empty account information. Sara cursed.

"Obviously you won't be any help," she sighed. "There's always my account."

She tasted fear just thinking about it. If she accessed her account now, Hank Allen could get wind of it. She might as well send him a flyer announcing that she had faked her own death.

Unless there were money trees in Texas, she was running out of options. There had to be a way for her to get the money without anyone knowing she was still alive.

"Assuming I still have any money," she said. "I *am* supposed to be dead. But Hank Allen doesn't know my banking information, so no one will have told the bank I'm dead."

She went to her bank's Web site and accessed her account information. Three hundred and sixteen dollars was sitting there. It wasn't a lot, but it would cover the costs of creating a new identity.

"How can a dead woman make a withdrawal?"

Irritated, she tapped her finger on the table. Then inspiration struck. "I can't. but the bank can do it for me. I am a genius!"

She had designed an automated billing system for Justin's patients. All she had to do was create a predated medical bill, then log in and tell her bank to pay it. If by some strange turn of events Hank Allen knew about her account, he wouldn't be suspicious of a medical bill from the area where she supposedly died. The only possible glitch was if he knew the bank required authorization for payment.

"Who am I kidding?" she scoffed with disdain. Hank Allen's accountant took care of all his finances. He was the same compliant little man who had doled out her allowance when she'd been married to Hank Allen, and signed the alimony checks that came later. Besides, this account was one she had opened after her divorce. Hank Allen would have to go through the motions of becoming the executor of her estate before he could access her account. With luck, he hadn't done that in the preceding three weeks.

Using another patient as a guide, Sara went into her account and arranged an automatic payment based on the dummied bill from Justin Dale, M.D. She did vary the information slightly. Instead of having the check sent to his office, she used the address of the guesthouse. She would have to forge his name when the check arrived, but she could only add that to her list of things to atone for once she was safely away.

She had left her real life behind without regret. Yet as she sat alone in the guesthouse, she acknowledged that leaving Cactus Creek would be difficult. The notion of never seeing Justin again filled her with melancholy.

Justin made her feel things she hadn't dreamed were possible. More important, she wasn't afraid of him on any level. He was the first man she had ever met that she felt truly comfortable with. She respected him. She definitely lusted for him. Mostly, she trusted him.

The worst part was, she would never know if they were meant to be together. She had woven herself into a web of lies that he would never forgive. How could he?

After shutting down the computer, Sara was careful to stash her notes inside her purse. All she had to do now was wait for the check to come. Soon she would be a whole new person. A person without Justin Dale in her life.

That wasn't what she wanted. But she didn't have a choice. It would have been nice to see if she was capable of a normal relationship. Explore the possibility of actually being loved.

"Whoa!" she warned herself. "Giant leap to be thinking about love."

Besides, she wasn't even sure she knew what that meant. Maybe she was confusing desire with a more important emotion. Perhaps she just wanted to enjoy the feelings he inspired.

"What's the harm in that?" she wondered aloud. "After all the years of abuse...the long struggle to build a life for myself, only to have Hank Allen derail me again. Would it be so terrible to make the best of my limited time with Justin?"

These question-and-answer periods with herself were growing annoying. She was getting antsy. Being cooped up wasn't doing her much good. She was getting way too analytical. For years, all she had allowed herself to want was peace and simplicity. To be able to do the things a normal woman in her twenties did. Find a nice little apartment. Get a decent job. Make some friends.

What a difference a month could make. Or more accurately, what a difference a kiss could make. Her vision of her future had never included a man. She touched her fingers to her lips. She remembered every blissful second of his kiss. She remembered the thrill of his touch. She remembered the feelings he had stirred.

Unfortunately, she also remembered it was all based on a lie.

CHAPTER TWELVE

SHE HEARD the car outside at the same time the phone
rang the following morning. Sara peered out at the
reassuring sight of the deputy's cruiser, then reached
for the receiver.

"Hello?"

Her voice was greeted by a series of faint clicks.

"Hello?" she repeated, uneasiness creeping into
her tone. Someone was on the other end. Someone
who wasn't talking. She slammed the phone back on
its cradle and dashed toward the door. Luckily, she
was able to flag down the deputy before he circled
toward town.

His tires spit dust and gravel as he backed up to
the front of the guesthouse. She wasn't exactly com-
forted when he stepped from the car, looping a night-
stick into his belt on the third attempt.

The guy looked about twelve. He had more acne
than facial hair and he wasn't what she would call of
imposing stature.

"Yes, ma'am? Is there a problem?"

"Someone just called."

"Who?"

"I don't know."

Removing his hat, the young man scratched the crown of his nearly-shaven head. "It could have been a wrong number, ma'am."

"Or it could be the man trying to kill me," she prompted in a less-than-gentle tone. "I need you to do something."

"I can make a report."

She shook her head when what she really wanted to do was shake the pencil-necked officer standing there with that vacant look in his narrow eyes. "Deputy—" she glanced down at his nameplate "—Ferrel, if that was Jeb Parker on the phone, it means he knows where I am."

"And the phone number, too," the deputy deduced, grinning, as if that was a major Sherlock Holmes moment in his career.

"If he knows all that, then making a report won't help."

"But I'm supposed to write up all of my incidents. It's regulation."

"I need help *now,* so I don't really care if your regulations are part of the terms of the Geneva Convention."

He gave her a goofy smile. "You must be confused, ma'am. We don't get no conventions here."

Closing her eyes, she said a silent prayer for patience. "Deputy Ferrel, listen to me carefully."

"Yes, ma'am."

"Do you know who I am?"

"Not really. All I know is that I'm supposed to do

a drive-by—that's what we call it in law enforcement when we go past a location on patrol.''

"Thank you for that tidbit, Sergeant Friday.''

"It's Ferrel, ma'am, not Friday,'' he corrected with a bashful smile. "And I'm not a sergeant. But I do have an application in with the Texas Rangers. Do you know they're one of the oldest law enforcement agencies in the United States of America?''

"Do you know how to focus?'' she fairly screamed.

The deputy looked offended. "I was just trying to explain, so as you would know I'm not a sergeant. I work for the sheriff, that makes me a deputy. You can't be a sergeant when you work for the sheriff. I wouldn't want you to get the wrong idea about my position or anything.''

"Deputy Ferrel,'' she began, enunciating clearly, "there is a man who has threatened to kill me.''

"Yeah, right,'' he said as if he'd just remembered. He slipped his hand into his uniform pocket and took out a photograph. He looked at it, then passed it to her. "Jeff Parker. Sheriff says we're all supposed to be on the lookout for him.''

"*Jeb* Parker.'' Sara stared down at the photograph. It was a color mug shot of a fierce-looking man holding numbers at his chest. He had dark hair, dark eyes and a dark scowl. It was her first real glimpse of Jeb Parker. Alec had shown her a similar photo, but it had been a fax, so it hadn't been as crisp and clear.

"I need you to take me into town.''

"We aren't allowed to take civilians for rides, ma'am."

She reached out and took him by the wrist, leading him inside. "Let's call the sheriff."

The deputy stood idly by as she called the number Justin had taped to the front of one of the kitchen cabinets. It was answered on the second ring.

"Younger here."

"Sheriff, it's Molly." Simply hearing a familiar voice was reassuring. "I got a call."

"He made contact?"

"There was someone on the other end, but all I could hear was some faint clicking and heavy breathing."

"Did you hit star sixty-nine when you hung up?"

Sara slapped her forehead. "I forgot you could retrieve the last number called. Sorry."

"No matter. I'll come right now."

"Deputy Ferrel is here," she told him, casting a glance in the direction of the underling. "I've been trying to get him to help out, but he seems a little…confused."

Alec laughed derisively. "Dumb as dryer lint, I hired him as a favor to my aunt Lizzy. Put him on the line."

Sara held out the receiver. "He wants to talk to you."

She saw the young man's Adam's apple bob beneath the loose-fitting collar of his shirt. His end of the conversation was little more than a series of "yes, sirs'' and ''no sirs.'' When he hung up, his face was flushed and blotchy.

''You're to come with me, ma'am. I'll be escorting you back to the station.''

It was obvious that Alec had taught him the sentence during their call. She was pretty sure *escorting* wasn't part of this guy's regular vocabulary.

Sara was uneasy during the drive to town, even though she was in a police cruiser. The only conversation she had with the deputy was to plead with him not to turn on the lights and sirens. He was actually pouting because she didn't want to draw any attention to herself.

As they drove along the unpaved road from the guesthouse, Sara recognized the pond off to the left. She had it noticed her first drive out to the guesthouse. It wasn't that big, but it had a pretty white bridge arching across the middle and a gazebo off to one side.

Soon two more buildings came into view. One was a barn or a stable. She wasn't sure of the correct term. A trio of horses stood in an adjacent pasture. One was huge and black and beautiful. The other two were shades of chestnut. None of them bothered to stop grazing as the car passed by.

The other building was a house—Justin's home. It was old, but meticulously maintained. The lawn was landscaped and there were even some hearty flowers still in bloom in pots on either side of the entryway.

It was two stories with lots of bright white trim to

contrast the blue-gray clapboards. It even had a picket fence around it. A dream house, she thought.

It took another five minutes before she realized they were coming up to the clinic. The deputy came to the main street and turned left. A few blocks later, he parked at the curb in front of a stately granite building. Municipal Center was spelled out in large stone letters above the columned facade.

Alec Younger was waiting for them at the top of the well-worn steps.

He dismissed the deputy and took Sara's arm, guiding her into the building. It was chilly inside and the sound of her thudding cast echoed through the empty hall.

She smelled stale smoke and coffee, odors that became stronger as they reached an office door with the words Sheriff's Department painted against opaque glass.

Once inside his office, Alec helped her into a chair across from a cluttered desk.

"You okay?" he asked.

"Winded," she admitted. "Dragging around ten pounds of cast is an aerobic workout."

"Want some water?"

She stared at him, trying to decipher why he was using such a detached tone. "Are you annoyed that I called?"

He sat in a high-backed, well-worn leather chair behind the desk. It squeaked as he leaned back, his eyes fixed on hers. "Nope."

She saw the challenge in his gaze. "You're annoyed that I exist."

He smiled an acknowledgment. "You're pretty perceptive for a woman who claims to have no memory."

Bracing her palms on the cold metal arms of her chair, Sara eased herself up. "I don't need this, sheriff. I called you for help, which obviously was a mistake."

"Sit down."

She stood still, refusing to follow his order.

"Please?" he amended, his tone only slightly more conciliatory.

She complied, but only because it was awkward and a little painful to have most of her weight on her one good leg. "You don't like me, do you?"

He shrugged. "Not relevant to my job."

"I think you dislike me on a personal level that has nothing to do with your job. I would like to know why."

"Let's just say I'm not as gullible as Justin."

Sara scoffed. "Justin doesn't strike me as the least bit gullible."

"He is where you're concerned."

"He's my doctor, Sheriff. Why does that get your gun in a knot?"

The sheriff took out a cigarette, lit it, and inhaled deeply. He was at least polite enough to blow the stream of blue smoke toward the ceiling.

"He's my best friend."

"Then I wish you both a long and happy friendship. But that still doesn't explain why you dislike *me*. You don't even know me."

"Instinct," Alec admitted without apology. "There's something about you that isn't right, *Mrs.* Parker."

"But aren't you supposed to be concerning yourself with *Mr.* Parker? Or are you one of those types who think a woman drives a man to beat her?"

"Don't think that for a second," he assured her. "If I got to make the rules, I'd sleep easy at night after locking up for good any man who raised a hand to a woman."

"That's a great speech, Sheriff, but I think you need a refresher course in sensitivity training. I'm the victim here. I don't need your hostility, and just so you know, I resent it like the hell."

His eyes conveyed just a tinge of respect. "Fair enough. I've requested the LUDs for the guesthouse from the phone company."

"LUDs?"

"Local usage details. I'll know the number and location of where the call was made inside an hour."

"Thank you," she said, tilting her head in acknowledgment. "Then what?"

"We find out where your husband is and arrest him for violating the restraining order."

"What about the beating? Won't he be charged with that?"

Alec shrugged. "Not unless you can remember details and testify to them in court."

"You said they found blood in the apartment. That the neighbors heard an argument and then I was gone."

"Hearsay," Alec explained. "He can get as much as a year in lockup for violating the court order, but he can't be prosecuted for assault without your testimony."

"I can't testify," she told him. It was the truth. She hadn't been there.

"For the record, I don't dislike you. I dislike the fact that my best friend is jumping headfirst into a mess. I don't want to see him hurt."

"Neither do I."

The sheriff moved closer, his gaze level. "You really don't remember anything, Mrs. Parker?"

She leaned forward, holding his gaze. "I'll swear on as many bibles as you can drag in here that I have absolutely no memory of the man or the marriage."

Alec blinked first. "Fair enough. Maybe my instincts are wrong this once, Mrs. Parker."

"Stop calling me that!" she snapped. "Molly is fine, and hearing it doesn't remind me that a crazy man wants to kill me."

"I'm not trying to antagonize you, but you've got to admit that this whole situation is pretty strange."

"It's absurd," she agreed easily. "It also isn't my fault."

"I am aware of that."

''Then why don't you do us both a favor and get that chip off your shoulder?''

Alec took another long pull on his cigarette. ''The doc and I go way back.''

''So you've said.''

''His folks took me in. Let me work as a hand on their ranch. Back then, the Dale family had one of the largest ranches in the county.''

''Sounds like a lovely, caring family and you were a lucky guy.''

''They were and I was. Justin was a late-in-life baby. By the time we were in our late teens, his folks were already too old to run cattle and they knew Justin wanted to be a doctor, not a rancher.''

''Is there a point to all this?''

''Yes. They sold off the stock to pay for Justin's education. His mama passed on in his freshman year. His dad joined her a year later. Most folks think he died of loneliness.''

''This is very touching, but it really isn't any of my business.''

Ignoring her interruption, Alec continued, ''Justin kept a sizable piece of the ranch for himself and sold the rest. Parceled the land free and clear for the clinic. Built it all with his own money so folks around here could have decent medical care.''

Feeling as if she were hearing tales out of school, Sara asked, ''Why are you telling me this?''

''Because I want you to know the kind of man

Justin is and because I don't want you screwing up his life.''

She was about to mount a defense when a radio crackled to life. The sheriff lifted the handset and acknowledged Deputy Ferrel.

"Go ahead, Billy."

"I'm here at Dr. Dale's guesthouse. I remembered that Mrs. Parker didn't take her purse when we left. I know women are real particular about having their purses with them so—"

"Get to the point, Billy," the sheriff interrupted, annoyed.

"I think you best come out here," the deputy said excitedly.

Frustrated, the sheriff asked, "Can't find her purse?"

"Um, it isn't about the purse. There's something here I think you should see."

CHAPTER THIRTEEN

HER RETURN to the guesthouse did include blaring sirens and flashing lights. It was a quick and bumpy trip that ended with the sheriff screeching to a stop so abruptly that the car slid uncontrolled for an instant.

"Put your gun in your holster before you shoot yourself, Billy," Alec groaned as he exited the cruiser. "What has you all riled up?"

Sara had joined the two men. Just as she had refused Alec's suggestion that she stay back at his office, she also refused to sit alone out in the open.

"In the kitchen." Billy's voice gushed with excitement as he rushed them inside.

Sara's eyes immediately saw what had spooked the young deputy. Bloodred paint had been sprayed on the refrigerator door. Five simple, yet chilling, words.

She felt dizzy and reached out to steady herself. Unfortunately, she was too far from the wall and ended up crumpling to a heap on the floor.

With unexpected compassion, Alec came to her aid, lifting her up and depositing her on the couch.

"Call for the Crime Scene Unit from your radio and then stay outside."

"Why?" Billy whined. "I was the first officer on the scene. I'm supposed to be in charge until the crime-scene unit arrives."

"Billy, I'll be in charge of kicking your ass if you don't go out there and do what I told you. Now! Move!"

Billy was still muttering complaints under his breath as he obeyed. Obviously, he had left the door open, because the red-and-blue lights from the cruiser were strobing around the room.

The sheriff stayed at her side, offering suggestions about taking deep breaths. She did as instructed, but it only seemed to be making her more light-headed.

She heard the sheriff let out a string of expletives. "Slower, you're hyperventilating."

"Make…up…your…mind!" Sara snapped. *This couldn't be happening.*

It took ten minutes for her to get her breathing back to normal. Seeing the words had shaken her to the core. These last few weeks had lulled her into a false sense of security. She obviously had more to fear from Jeb Parker than she had thought.

"You can't go in there!"

She turned toward the sound of the deputy's wailing voice. Ferrel was a stride behind Justin.

"Are you okay?"

He knelt before her, automatically searching for signs of injury. When he took her hands, she realized his were trembling. He looked at her with concern and something more. In the dark depths of those chocolate eyes, she knew instantly that his feelings for her were genuine. Instinctively, she knew they went beyond mere casual friendship. It was as if she could see into his soul. But neither his soul nor his feelings could protect her from Jeb Parker.

Justin leaned over and kissed the top of her head before standing and turning to the sheriff. "What the hell happened? I damn near crashed when I saw the emergency lights from the air."

Alec crooked his head in the direction of the refrigerator. "Seems Parker has finally surfaced and I think he's pissed."

"Did he hurt you?" Justin asked.

She shook her head. "I wasn't here."

"Where the hell were you?"

"At the sheriff's office." She calmed him somewhat when she recounted the events of the morning.

Justin felt like punching something. More accurately, he felt like punching *someone*. What kind of man could write You Are a Dead Bitch in red paint?

Justin paced the small space between the sofa and the fireplace. He didn't like feeling so useless. It rankled to think he could resuscitate a dead person, yet he couldn't manage to keep one woman safe from a psycho.

"Get your things," he said to Molly.

"Hang on," Alec interjected. "This is a police matter, Justin. Let me handle it."

"Get your things," he repeated. "I'm taking Molly

to the house. Park a deputy there twenty-four hours a day. And not that idiot outside.''

Alec grabbed his arm. ''I'm the cop, you're the doctor. Let me handle this.''

For the first time since they were teenagers, Justin came close to slugging the man who was like a brother to him. Their eyes locked and Justin silently warned his friend off. Reluctantly, Alec let go.

''Think this through, Doc.''

''There's nothing to think about. She can't be alone.''

''Agreed. But let me take care of her. I'll find someplace to stash her until we find Parker. Now that we know he's in the area, there are only so many places he can hide.''

''She'll be safe with me.''

''I don't think so. Parker found the guesthouse so he must know about you. How long do you think it will take before he goes looking for her at your place?''

''I hope he does,'' Justin rasped in a burst of anger.

''Do I get to join this conversation?'' Molly asked.

''No!''

''No!'' Justin repeated a split second behind his friend.

Alec was glaring at him. ''You're going about this all wrong, Doc. This isn't your fight.''

''I'm making it mine.''

''Then you're making a mistake,'' Alec cautioned. ''We don't know what Parker is capable of.''

"Yes, we do," Justin seethed. "I counted several previous breaks in her arm, one in her jaw, and possible skull fractures, and that's not including the injuries she had when she was brought in."

"I can protect her," Alec reasoned.

"So can I," Justin countered.

"It's my job."

"Not anymore."

"What are you going to do if he shows, Doc?"

"My guess is he won't show up with a marked car in front of my place. He knows there's a warrant out on him."

Justin knew Alec was thinking. He got a kind of faraway look in his eyes and you could almost hear the gears grinding.

"He didn't bite on any of the phony motel registrations," Alec said aloud. "There's enough abandoned barns, sheds and fields in this part of Texas for him to hide for a good long while."

"So we draw him out?" Justin asked, catching his friend's train of thought.

"Might be the fastest way," Alec suggested.

"No thank you," Molly chimed in. "There is no way in this big world that I'm going to be used like bait so you can catch this creep."

Justin leveled his gaze on her. "Don't you want him behind bars?"

"Of course."

"Got a better suggestion?"

"Roadblocks, APBs, old-fashioned police work?"

''None of that has worked so far,'' Justin said pointedly. ''Do you want this over?''

''Of course.''

''Then let's work out a plan.''

''I LIKED MY plan better,'' Sara grumbled as she followed him inside the two-story house she had admired earlier in the day. ''Alec liked my plan better, too.''

''Too risky,'' Justin said. ''And Alec's only objection was because he doesn't think the two of us staying under one roof is a good idea.''

''Is he your conscience or your friend?''

''Both,'' Justin told her with a wink. ''C'mon, I'll give you the grand tour.''

''I don't think this is a good idea, Justin. I could go to a motel and the deputies can keep watch over me.'' *And I'll be able to slip away so you don't find out I'm not Molly Parker.*

''We've been over this,'' Justin warned. ''We have to draw Parker out into the open. The deputies will watch over you here when I'm at the clinic during the day. They'll be parked out front all night, every night, until your husband is in custody. The rest of the time, I'm going to stick to you like glue.''

I doubt you'll stick around when you find out I'm an imposter, she thought as she followed him through the foyer. *Lord, have I ever dug myself in deep. I have to figure a way out of this mess before it gets any worse.* How much worse could it get? She didn't dare speculate, not the way her luck was running.

Justin walked ahead of her. Or more accurately, he had this kind of sexy swagger, she thought, admiring his broad shoulders, tapered waist and long, muscled legs. She was an idiot! Why on earth was she lusting after this man? The answer was obvious—it was impossible not to.

The best way she could think to describe Justin's house was homey. There were several doors off the foyer, and after glancing through the first one, she guessed these rooms hadn't been altered in years. Somehow Justin didn't seem like the kind of guy to have decided on a formal Victorian parlor. The second room she looked into on the opposite side of the hallway seemed more manly. Like the guesthouse, it was decorated with heavy mahogany furniture. A huge desk dominated the space, complete with intricate carvings around the claw-and-ball feet. The chairs were also oversize, and covered in brown leather. The only thing she could see that dated past the nineteenth century was a state-of-the-art computer.

They passed a staircase guarded by matching newel posts that had been crafted to resemble miniature lions' heads. The house was shadowy, probably because the only lighting in the hallway was a single fixture. There were sconces on the walls but they looked as if they had never made the conversion from oil to electricity.

They ended up in a rectangular room that had a much more modern feel to it. Careful inspection showed that a wall had been removed, opening the kitchen area into what was originally designed as a family parlor.

Much of the back wall was glass, revealing an incredible view of the pond and gazebo off in the distance.

"This is breathtaking," she said, only then realizing that she had spoken her thoughts aloud.

"It's pretty peaceful," he agreed as he tossed a small duffel that held all her worldly possessions on the floor next to a tiled cooking island.

Sara took in the Sub-Zero refrigerator, the double ovens and indoor grill, and more gadgets than she had ever seen outside a culinary specialty store, then looked to Justin for some sort of explanation.

"I let a decorator make a few of the decisions during the remodeling. The old kitchen still had a wood-burning stove and a freezer that only worked during certain phases of the moon."

"This is a pretty elaborate setup," she stated as she moved to a stool at the cooking island and tried to climb up.

"Let me help," Justin offered.

He placed one hand on either side of her waist and gently assisted her onto the stool. That was all it took.

As if reading her thoughts, Justin rhetorically asked, "I shouldn't have touched you, right?"

"Right."

The smart move would be to push him away. But her IQ was dropping almost as fast as her blood pressure was rising.

"I didn't think one kiss would be enough," he drawled. His voice was deep, low and sensual.

She didn't argue. She couldn't. She felt exactly the same way. Having him within reach, feeling his hands on her body easily erased all other things from her mind. Well, save for one thing.

Brazenly, she lifted a tentative hand to his cheek. His skin was slightly rough and deeply tanned. Her fingers looked small and pale as she followed the line of his jaw. The pad of her forefinger danced across his lower lip. She felt him tense, felt his grip tighten at her sides. Once again, the heady blend of power and control pressed her on.

Leaving his mouth for the moment, she used both hands and began to explore the vast expanse of his chest.

"Molly?"

"Yes."

"This isn't a good idea."

"I think it is." She managed to work his tie free. Slowly, she released the top button of his shirt. She heard his ragged breath, felt it rush against her face. He smelled of soap and cologne.

Leaning forward, Sara placed a feather-soft kiss against the springy hair she had uncovered.

"Molly?"

"Hush." She worked the second button free and

then the next, kissing every inch until she had tugged the shirt free from his jeans.

"We can't do this," Justin said.

"I thought it was women who had the reputation for saying no when they really meant yes."

Justin crooked one finger under her chin and lifted her face to his. His eyes were positively smoldering. Seeing them sent a shiver down her spine that radiated to every other cell in her body.

"I'm trying really hard to be gallant here."

"Why?" She took his hand from under her chin and kissed each fingertip in turn.

Justin made a guttural sound that was some blend of a moan and a groan. "You are making this impossible."

"Good. That was my goal."

His head fell back and she heard him take in a gulp of air when she slipped the tip of one finger into her mouth. She was about to do the same to the others when she was suddenly swooped off the stool.

She was on her back on the sofa before she even had time to take a breath. Justin's mouth covered hers, as did his body—or at least it seemed to. In fact, her leg with the cast was braced on the floor, and much of Justin's weight was resting on the cushions beneath his knees.

He wasn't kissing her, he was devouring her. The raw passion of it overwhelmed her. Her hands raked his hair. Justin seemed to know exactly when to apply pressure, and when to pull back. When to nibble her lip and when to resume the kiss.

The sound of her own rapidly beating heart echoed in her ears. She almost didn't hear the small gasp fall from her lips when his hand slipped beneath her shirt.

It was a slow, deliberate upward exploration. He took his time, stroking the curve of her waist, then her side, always careful not to do anything more than brush the fabric of her bra. It was more sensual than actually being touched. But that didn't seem to matter. Her whole body ached to feel his hand close on her breast. It was all she could seem to think about. She felt a thrilling urgency and need pulsing through her veins.

"Touch me," she said against his mouth when she could no longer bear the teasing.

The flimsy fabric of her blouse was unable to shield her from the heat emanating from his large body. She felt the roughness of his chest hair as he shifted positions. Sara was tugging at his shirt, pushing it down over his well-developed biceps.

Justin made some sort of primal sound as he pulled his hand away long enough to shake one arm free of his shirt. She felt his fingers working the buttons of her blouse, then cool air against her flushed skin. Then she felt him. He kissed her again, deeply. The kind of kiss that reached the knot of need in her stomach.

It seemed an eternity before her dream was realized. Justin's palm closed over her silk-clad breast.

He didn't grope or knead. He had this amazing ability to know just how to touch her. Her body responded almost instantly. His thumb gently teased her nipple erect. It was an amazing, mind-numbing blend of erotic sensations. Her body felt as if it was on fire.

Justin lifted his head as he shifted some of his weight onto one side. His hooded eyes began a frank and open perusal of her body. It was as intimate as his touch.

"You're beautiful," he murmured when his mouth found her neck. She arched slightly, needing to feel as much of him as possible.

His mouth burned a path down her throat, then lower. She gasped when his teeth toyed with the lace edging of her bra. She grabbed his head and pulled him against her. Justin taunted her nipple through the fabric. She could feel his hot breath through the silk barrier. He was making her crazy!

When he gently sucked, she grasped his shoulders and felt her fingernails meet sinewy muscle. It wasn't enough. She wanted more. And she wanted it immediately.

She began to yank at his shirt, her actions frantic. Justin must have sensed what she wanted, because he pulled back and caught her hands in his.

She felt his ragged breath against her face. Saw the flush of desire on his cheeks. When she lifted her eyes to his, she went motionless.

"What did I do wrong?" she asked.

Justin rolled off the sofa and had his arm back in

his shirtsleeve before she could even register what was happening.

His back was to her so she could see his breathing was still labored. She could also hear the rustle of fabric as he rebuttoned his shirt.

Modesty dictated that she follow suit. Quickly, she fastened most of the buttons and pushed her completely mussed hair out of her face.

"Are you going to tell me what I did?"

Justin didn't turn around. "What makes you think you did anything wrong."

Because Hank Allen said it to me often enough. "Well, you jumped away from me like your life depended on it."

Slowly, he turned, his face composed except for a few tiny beads of perspiration on his brow. "I got up because in another second or so, I wouldn't have been able to."

Sara dropped her gaze. "Okay. I understand."

"Do you?" he demanded, clearly annoyed.

She was an expert on the subject of not wanting to have sex with someone. It had been a hallmark of her marriage. "Sure, you had a change of heart. It happens."

"A change of heart?" he fairly sneered. "You think I suddenly didn't want you?"

"It's okay, really. I misread where we were headed. Let's not belabor the point."

"You read it perfectly."

She lifted her eyes to meet his. "Then I suppose I

don't understand why you suddenly decided to put the brakes on.''

"It became obvious that you weren't going to.''

"Oh, please!" she snapped. All that unspent passion seemed to transform into an anger she hadn't known was a part of her personality. "Who made it my responsibility? Especially since you were acting like a willing participant.''

He glared at her but she was unmoved.

"You have absolutely no reason to be angry at me. As I recall, I wasn't the one who moved the action to the sofa.''

"But you know how I feel. I live by a code of principles. Of rules.''

"Well, I have a news flash for you, doctor. You only seem to drag out your rules and principles when they're convenient for you. So to make things easier for both of us, I'll make a new rule.''

"Really?''

"Yes. Keep your hands to yourself unless you plan to follow through.''

His expression darkened. "That's a good rule, but I doubt you could enforce it.''

"Meaning?''

He stepped closer and leaned toward her ear. In a soft but determined tone he whispered, "You want me, Molly. And I want you. I don't think it would take a tremendous effort to get you into bed.''

She shoved him away. "You're probably right. But at least I'm honest about it.''

CHAPTER FOURTEEN

"I CAN'T BELIEVE THIS," Julie said, rushing forward to meet him.

Dylan enveloped her in his arms. "My God. It's really you. I've been looking for you for so long," he whispered against her hair.

Julie's joy at seeing Dylan suddenly evaporated. Pushing him back to arm's length, she asked, "Did Sebastian send you?"

"No," Dylan replied quickly, his hands moving to cup her upturned face. "I can't believe this, either. I was starting to think you really were dead."

Cautiously, Julie asked, "Are you sure Sebastian doesn't know I'm here? He isn't following you?"

Dylan frowned. "Of course not. I came here to find a Dr. Dale. I was told he treated the woman who was with Sara Pierce when she died."

Julie blinked. "How do you know Sara Pierce?"

"I don't," Dylan answered. "I was hired to find the heirs to an estate of a woman in Pinto. Sara Pierce was one of them. I tracked her as far as the Harrisons' shelter. So I guess now I'm looking for her heirs. I heard there was an ex-husband."

Julie reached up and traced her finger along his

jawline. Seeing him again was like a dream come true. It also reminded her of the nightmare she'd left behind.

"What happened?" Dylan asked.

Julie turned and waved her hand in the direction of the crib.

"Yours?" Dylan asked.

She nodded as she watched Dylan move over to the crib and admire her sleeping baby.

"He's beautiful, Julie."

She smiled with maternal pride. "No argument from me. He's a wonderful blessing."

"Is he okay?"

"He's recovering from pneumonia," she told him. "For a while, I thought I might lose him."

Dylan draped his arm around her shoulder. "Why didn't you get in touch with me?"

"I was afraid."

"Of me?"

Julie met his gaze. "I wasn't sure whose side you were on." She led him to the desk, sat him in a chair, then leaned against the edge of the desk. She thought for a moment before she spoke. "Sebastian is involved with the mob."

"Do you know that for sure?"

Julie rubbed her face. "I know it sounds incredible, but it's true."

"Do you have proof?"

She nodded. "But you don't sound completely surprised?"

"Let's just say I had my suspicions. But tell me what you know. God, Julie, I still can't believe it's you."

She squeezed his hand, then thought back to that January day one year ago. "You know we were trying to have a baby, right?"

Dylan nodded, his eyes locked with hers.

"I saw Dr. Klein secretly," Julie went on, "because I wasn't sure if I was pregnant or not, and after the miscarriage, I wanted to be sure before I said anything to Sebastian. When Dr. Klein confirmed I was pregnant, I rushed over to tell him."

"I know. Hector saw you come into the building, but not leave. And Sebastian denies you were ever there."

Blowing out a breath, Julie said, "Let me back up a minute. When I got to Sebastian's office, his secretary was out and so was he. I decided to hide in the bathroom in his office and pop out to surprise him. I'd barely stepped inside when I heard Sebastian come back to his office—he was arguing with someone."

"But Hector said you were the only one to see Sebastian that morning," Dylan objected.

Julie shook her head. "Hector was mistaken. I was terrified when I heard their conversation."

"Which was?" Dylan prompted.

"I couldn't catch every word. I just know that they were both angry and discussing J. B. Crowe and something about a kidnapping."

"And that made you think Sebastian was involved with the mob?"

She groaned. "Why else would they be talking about J. B. Crowe? Even I know his reputation—and I read about his arrest last spring."

"Did you catch the guy's name?" Dylan asked.

She shook her head. "I'm not even sure Sebastian called him by name. But I know for sure it wasn't some sort of innocent business meeting. Sebastian's involved with the mob. I *know* it."

"Do you have any hard proof?"

Julie shook her head. "No. That's why I ran. I was afraid for my baby's safety."

"We're talking about your husband," Dylan said. "Do you really think he would have harmed his own son?"

"No," Julie said honestly. "Though I was the one who wanted the baby. But by getting involved with mobsters, he was putting all of our lives at risk."

When Dylan didn't say anything, Julie pressed him. "Do you find it so hard to believe Sebastian could be involved in something illegal?"

Dylan shrugged. "I'm not sure what to think. I saw Sebastian with one of Crowe's men a while back. I have to admit it made me uneasy. And he's been acting so strange—his moods are so erratic—but I passed it off as worry over you."

Julie looked skeptical. "It's more likely worry about himself."

"He was really devastated, Julie, especially when you first disappeared. Lately he seems...haunted."

Julie's eyebrows drew together. "What's haunting him is of his own making."

"You didn't have any inkling of this before that morning?" Dylan asked.

Vehemently, Julie shook her head. "I didn't have a clue." She felt frustration grip her. "I wish I had, Dylan. It's as if my whole life is a sham. Like nothing was ever real. All I know is that I can never trust Sebastian again. I know that with every fiber of my being—and I can never risk my baby's life by going back."

Dylan stood and pulled her into his arms. Julie allowed her face to rest against his chest. She felt safe in his embrace. His quiet strength worked wonders on her frazzled emotions. Not for the first time, Julie thought about the mistake she had made. She had always loved Dylan. He was more than a friend. She should have told him the truth before ever marrying Sebastian. Then she wouldn't be suffering through all the what-ifs.

Dylan stroked her hair as he asked, "What have you been doing all this time?"

She sighed. "Where do I begin. I didn't want to endanger my father, so I couldn't go to Wisconsin. Instead I hitched a ride with a trucker—"

"Hitchhiked?"

"It seemed prudent at the time. Anyway, I traveled around for a while, then I went to Louisiana to see an old friend. Sebastian doesn't know anything about her as far as I know—she's kind of a Cajun version of a midwife.''

"She helped you with the birth?"

"Yes."

"That explains why I couldn't find any records of you giving birth. I had feelers out in every hospital in the state."

She patted his chest. "I was afraid Sebastian would find me that way. Anyway, I had to conserve my money, so I gave her my mother's locket in exchange for her services."

"So how did you end up in Cactus Creek? And why did you take out those personal ads in the San Antonio paper?"

She tilted her head up to meet his smiling eyes. "You knew it was me?"

He nodded. "I suspected. You're the only one who knows I peruse the personal ads for potential clients and I have a penchant for Dylan Thomas poetry."

"I wanted you to know I was okay, but was afraid to contact you directly. Sebastian is your best friend."

"*Was* my best friend," Dylan amended.

Julie heard the sadness in his voice and recalled her own reaction to discovering her husband's hidden life. It was almost as if Sebastian had died. At least the Sebastian she thought she knew was dead.

"I also wasn't sure you would believe me."

Dylan made a dismissive sound. "I believe you, I just wish I had something solid to take to the cops."

Julie gave a shudder. "I hate the thought of my son's father being a criminal. Thomas deserves better."

"Thomas?"

Julie smiled, feeling her cheeks warm. "A reference to my dearest friend's favorite poet." More than my dearest friend—the man I wish was my son's father.

"I'm touched, Julie," Dylan said, kissing the top of her head. "But I'm not so sure I like you as a brunette."

"Me, either," she admitted, stepping away from his embrace.

"How can I help you now that I've found you?" Dylan asked.

She shook her head. "There isn't anything anyone can do. And please, please promise me that you won't tell Sebastian where I am?"

"That goes without saying," Dylan replied. "But I'm not leaving you and the baby out here in the middle of nowhere."

"We're not staying here. Thomas is getting better."

"Shouldn't he be in a real hospital?"

Julie smiled. "Justin—Dr. Dale—is excellent. Thomas was never more than a helicopter flight away from a major hospital. Thankfully, Justin was able to treat him here for the most part. Whenever he needs any major tests we take him to Fort Worth. Justin bent a few rules since Thomas has no medical coverage."

"There has to be some way I can help," Dylan insisted. "I am going to leave you in better financial shape—don't argue. You can consider it a loan till we figure out how to get you safely out of here."

"I won't refuse the money, Dylan, but there is no way I can go back to San Antonio. I don't know enough to turn Sebastian over to the authorities and I won't risk my son's safety."

"Now that I have an idea of what to look for, maybe I can get enough evidence to—" Dylan paused to swallow the difficult thought "—put Sebastian in jail."

"It seems incredible, doesn't it?"

Dylan agreed with a subtle nod. "But it does explain a few things that have been pecking at my brain these past few moments."

"How long can you stay?" Julie asked.

It was Dylan's turn to sigh. "Not long. Not without risking Sebastian calling the office and being told I'm in Cactus Creek. He knows I'm still looking for you and I wouldn't want to do anything to make him suspicious."

"Please don't," Julie almost cried. "I don't want you to be in danger."

"I can take care of myself," he insisted. "I'm more worried about you and the baby."

"We're fine here," Julie insisted. "Thanks to Molly, there's a police car outside the clinic most of the time."

"Molly Parker?" Dylan asked.

"Yes."

"That's the woman I want to talk to," he explained. Dylan reached into his jacket pocket and pulled out a photograph. "This is the picture of Sara Pierce. I'm hoping Molly might have had a conversation with her when they were in the shelter together. It's a stretch, but I'd like to tie up the loose ends so I can finish this case."

Julie stared at the picture Dylan had provided. Very softly, she whispered, "Oh, my!"

"I WON'T cave in on this," Justin retorted, just a tad too smugly for her liking.

"Don't be too sure," she replied easily. "If you're finished taunting me, perhaps you'd be kind enough to show me to my room."

A glint sparkled in his dark eyes. "I don't taunt. I was simply stating a fact."

"I refuse to let you bait me, Justin. As far as I'm concerned, this is a closed subject. I'm immune to you as of this minute."

"No, you're not."

"Has anyone ever mentioned that you have an arrogant side?"

He laughed. "Occasionally. I'll take you upstairs."

"Can I trust you to be a gentleman?"

"Probably not, but for now, I'm content to wait until you come to me. On my terms."

"I didn't know we had terms. You don't negotiate, as I recall."

"I'll make an exception this time."

"So what are your terms?"

He gave her a slow, sensual grin. "Immune, huh?"

"Yes," she insisted with as much dignity as she could muster. "But I'm also curious."

"You don't want me to touch you unless I mean to finish the job, right?"

"A rather vulgar and simplistic way of saying it. But, correct."

"It is a fair request, so I'll agree to it. Now you have to agree to my stipulation."

"I won't agree to anything until I've heard it."

"You have," he said as he reached for her hand. "I told you last night. I have a rule against seducing married women. I don't want to start anything until you're divorced."

With his help, she stood on somewhat shaky legs. "Too late, Doc. You've already started something. Your problem seems to be finishing what you start."

"Cute, Molly. I'm serious, though."

She pulled her hand from his. "No, Justin. You're a hypocrite. Deep down you don't think of me as being married any more than I do. You got burned by a woman once, so you hide behind a set of rules and regulations to keep yourself from getting hurt again. But being safe means you never give anyone a chance to get close."

"You're hardly in a position to make proclamations about relationships."

You're wrong. I know exactly what you're feeling.

For years I've been afraid to let any man get close to me. Until you. But she couldn't tell him that. So she simply said, "We'll see."

Just as they reached the steps, the telephone rang. It gave Sara a start, and she held her breath until she heard Justin say hello to Julie.

"I'll make arrangements with Alec and be there as soon as possible."

"Is something wrong?" she asked when he had ended the conversation.

"Julie wants me to stay with the baby. She has some sort of urgent errand and Mrs. Beasley isn't available to monitor him on room air."

"Is Thomas okay?"

"I'm sure he's fine. But I should check in on him anyway. I dumped the two of them at the clinic to race to the guesthouse."

"So go," Sara insisted.

"I'm not leaving you alone."

"Your first responsibility is to your patient," she insisted.

Justin took her by the hand and led her into the masculine study. Reaching into his pocket, he produced a key ring and unlocked the gun cabinet on the far wall.

"I suppose it's pointless to ask if you know how to fire a gun."

"Yes. And get that away from me. I don't want any part of a gun."

He grabbed her hand and slapped the heavy metal

pistol in her palm. "It's simple, Molly. You just aim it and pull the trigger."

"Not likely."

"Would you prefer to let your husband beat you again? Or worse?"

"What about the deputy? Isn't there supposed to be someone outside?"

Justin grabbed the phone off the desk and made the call. When he was finished, he returned to where she was standing, the gun still flat in her palm and held as far away from her body as her arm would stretch.

"He's on his way. It will take ten minutes for the deputy to get here. That's enough time for you to get off one practice round."

"Shoot something?" she scoffed.

"This isn't up for debate."

She was about to open her mouth to contradict him when she read the unspoken plea in his eyes. "Okay. What do you want me to do?"

"Let's go out back."

Justin led her through the kitchen, passed a laundry room and out a side door. "See that tree?"

"You want me to shoot a tree?"

"It's the closest target available on this short notice."

He stood behind her, wrapping his arms around her so that his hands covered hers. Sara struggled to keep her mind on his instructions since it seemed to be more interested in the feel of his body pressed against hers.

"Look down the sight."

"That metal thingy at the end of the barrel?"

"Yes. Lock your elbows and apply even pressure on the trigger as you pull back."

Closing first one eye, then the second, she did as instructed, heard the pop, then was surprised when she felt the strong recoil and smelled the acrid scent of gunpowder.

"You can open your eyes now," Justin said.

Sara looked at the tree. Not a mark on it. "I told you this wasn't a good idea."

"Try again, only this time, watch the target."

"The *target* is a poor, defenseless tree."

"I can buy another tree."

Sara repeated the steps and amazed herself when she heard a snap and saw a small explosion of bark where the bullet skirted the trunk.

"I hit it!"

"That was the general idea," Justin teased. "You only nicked it, so I'm sure the tree will live a long and healthy life."

"Come back inside and I'll show you how to reload."

"I have to reload, too?"

"You should know how," Justin insisted as he led her back into the den.

From the desk drawer, he pulled out a cardboard box of bullets and a shiny metal object.

Taking the gun from her, he demonstrated how to release the clip. It clattered onto the floor. "Take the full clip and push it in, then pull back on the slide to load the chamber. Now you try.''

Sara took the gun and pressed the lever on the side and the metal clip fell to the floor. She retrieved it and pushed it back into place. "Satisfied?''

"You forgot to load the chamber. The gun won't fire unless you give it some bullets.''

"I'll remember,'' she promised.

Justin took the gun and snapped new bullets into one clip, then replaced the two she had fired from the other. He handed her the gun and both clips.

"Lock and load, as they say.''

Sara was very careful when she loaded the gun. Justin showed his appreciation with a satisfied smile. "Put the extra clip in your pocket.''

"How many bullets are in a clip?''

"In that model?'' he asked as he returned to the gun cabinet and took out a second, heavier weapon. "Each clip holds sixteen rounds.''

"No pun intended, but isn't thirty-two bullets overkill.''

He chuckled as he loaded his own weapon. "Better to be safe than sorry.'' He tucked the gun into the back of his waistband. "Keep that gun within reach at all times.''

"I will.''

She followed Justin to the door. He checked to verify that the marked car was in place before he turned and took her face in his hands. "Don't open this door for anyone.''

"I won't."

His gaze lingered for a second and his expression softened. "I'm sorry about earlier."

"Thank you. You really didn't have any reason to be mad at me."

"That's not what I'm apologizing for."

"Then what?"

"I'm sorry I didn't finish what I started."

"I AM IN a world of trouble," she mused as she considered tackling the stairs to explore the second floor. She was living proof that lies multiplied exponentially. Her hand was on the banister when she heard a knock at the door.

She experienced a flash of fear and took the gun from her back pocket, gripping it in both hands.

Cautiously, she went to the door and called, "Who is it?"

"It's Julie. Let me in."

She opened the door, then raised the gun when she saw the man standing behind Julie.

His hand snaked out and ripped the weapon from her hand before she even realized what he was doing.

"He's a friend," Julie explained in a rush. "Don't make the deputy suspicious, *Sara*."

"What did you call me?"

"Let's go inside," Julie suggested.

Sara hobbled back to the sofa and sat down.

Julie took a seat next to her and the man stood over

near the fireplace, one booted foot resting on the hearth as he gingerly placed her gun on the mantel.

"This is Dylan Garrett," Julie introduced. "He's an old friend of mine."

"I thought you weren't in touch with any of your friends."

"We'll get to that," Julie insisted. "But first I need to know the truth from you."

"What truth?"

Julie rolled her eyes. "Do you know who you really are? If your memory loss is real, then we need to have this conversation with Justin around."

She hung her head. "I am Sara Pierce."

"Thank God," Julie breathed.

Sara was surprised at the reaction. "You aren't furious at me for lying to you?"

Julie laughed. "I'm hardly in any position to pass judgment on your actions. And if what Dylan has told me is true, you had good reason to assume another woman's identity."

"Only *I* was dumb enough to pick a woman with a husband as vicious as my ex."

"Does Justin know?"

She shook her head vehemently. "And I can't possibly tell him the truth now."

"Why?"

Because I think I'm in love with him. "He's gone to so much trouble to try to help Molly Parker. He's involved the police and done all this stuff with motels and…" Her voice trailed off.

"Will you give us a minute, Dylan?" Julie asked.

When the quiet man disappeared into the den, Sara asked, "Who *is* he?"

"I went to college with Dylan. We've been friends for years."

"Doesn't that also make him a friend of your husband's? The one you're hiding from?"

Julie nodded. "But I trust him. You can, too."

"Trust him to do what?"

"He can help you. In fact, he came to Cactus Creek looking for you."

"You mean Molly Parker?"

"No. This is a little complicated."

"Confusing is more like it," Sara sighed.

"Dylan is a private detective."

"Jeb Parker hired him?"

"Mol—Sara," Julie caught herself and smiled. "I'm going to have to get used to calling you that. When Dylan showed up at the clinic this afternoon, I darn near fainted."

"Is Thomas okay?"

She nodded. "Of course. He's cranky from the trip to Fort Worth, but that worked to my advantage. It gave me a reason to get Justin away from here so we could talk."

"If Jeb Parker didn't hire your friend, then who did?"

"Dylan's agency was hired to find some heirs. You're one of them."

Sara blinked, more confused than ever. "That isn't

possible. I was raised in an orphanage. I don't have any relatives who would remember me in a will."

"Violet Mitchum?" Julie asked. "Do you know her?"

Sara nodded. "Kind of. I spoke with her very briefly in a hospital emergency room years ago. In fact, I was going to see her when the state trooper picked me up and took me to the shelter."

"I really should let Dylan explain all the details to you, but I want to know what you're going to do about Justin."

"Nothing."

"Sara!"

She threw her hands up in disgust. "There is only one thing I can do and I've already started that ball rolling." She explained to Julie about the new identity she planned to assume.

Julie listened patiently, then pointedly asked, "That's your solution?"

"Becoming Molly Parker has freed me from Hank Allen. Alec already told me my ex-husband refused to even claim my body. I can do the same thing with Jeb Parker. All I have to do is assume the identity of Emily Louise Ross."

"Don't you want to be yourself?" Julie asked. "Live a life where you aren't looking over your shoulder?"

"I tried that," Sara reminded her friend. "If Hank Allen finds out I'm alive, he'll find a way to get me."

"So have him arrested!" Julie pleaded.

"That gives me maybe eighteen months of tormented peace. Then he gets out and he's more determined than ever."

"So you're going to walk away from Justin?"

"No," Sara answered with a sarcasm aimed at herself. "I'm going to stay here and play house with him until he finds out I'm a liar."

"I don't think he wants to play," Julie opined. "I saw his face when we were landing. The man is in love with you."

"Which me, Julie? The Molly with no memory, or Sara Pierce the imposter, who has no ability to enter into a permanent relationship?"

"I think you should give him a chance to decide for himself."

She rubbed her face, feeling decades older than her true age. "But I don't have any options. If I go back to being Sara Pierce, I'd be putting Justin in more danger than I have already. At least now, if Jeb Parker shows up, he'll know I'm not his wife and probably slither away."

"Justin isn't a man who scares easily."

"You haven't seen Hank Allen in a rage."

Julie leaned closer. "Justin knows why I'm hiding from my husband. I had to tell him in order to keep him from transferring Thomas to a hospital in the city. The men who are after me are as bad—if not worse—than your ex-husband."

"I don't think there is such a creature."

"My husband is mixed up with organized crime."

Sara gaped at Julie. "You're a mob wife?"

Julie's mouth curved into a sad frown. "I guess so. But I didn't know that. I might not ever have known if I hadn't overheard a conversation I wasn't supposed to hear."

"But you're the mother of the man's son. Surely he wouldn't hurt you or Thomas."

"He'll never get close enough to Thomas." Julie's eyes filled with pain. "I went to his office to tell him I was pregnant. That's how I happened to hear the conversation."

Sara sighed wearily. "The two of us sure know how to pick men, don't we?"

"I can't fix my mistake yet," Julie said, her voice a mere whisper. "But once I have concrete evidence, I plan on making things right."

Sara digested her words for a moment, then asked, "Dylan?"

Julie nodded and light came pouring back into her eyes. "I should have married him. I've loved him since the dawn of time."

"So what stopped you?"

"He never asked. Instead of going after the man I really wanted, I settled for a man I thought I could be content with. Something tells me you're about to make the same mistake."

"I already married the wrong guy," Sara reminded her.

"Divorced him, too. Not that that did me any good." She went on to tell Julie about the years following her divorce, culminating with that ill-fated graduation day. "I did everything an abused woman is supposed to do. It wasn't enough to keep me safe then, and nothing has changed."

"You met Justin."

"Who I've lied to almost from the very start. Even if I told him everything, it couldn't work for us."

"Why?"

"Assuming he could forgive me—which is a pretty big assumption—do you really think he'd toss away his life here so that we could keep one step ahead of my ex-husband?"

"You're selling him short, Sara. If you give him a chance, I'm sure Justin would find a way for the two of you to have a future."

"Uh-huh."

Sara and Julie turned to find Dylan standing in the entryway clearing his throat.

"Sorry," Julie offered. "Come over and sit down. Sara needs your help."

He was an imposing man, with brown, sun-streaked hair that looked as if it could use a trim. He had intense blue eyes and laugh lines around his mouth, and his easygoing manner calmed some of Sara's trepidation.

"How did you find me?" she asked without preamble.

He shrugged. "I finally got a call back from your ex-husband a few days ago. He told me you had died in Pinto. When I got here, I conned an assistant at the sheriff's office into showing me the autopsy photos. You and Molly Parker share a resemblance, but I knew immediately that the dead woman wasn't you.''

''How? We've never met.''

''I got the superintendent to let me into your apartment. I found some pictures of you there.''

''You didn't tell anyone, did you?''

''Nope. I went back to the sheriff's assistant, who told me about the shelter where the body was found. The couple that run that place weren't forthcoming, so I had to go at it from another angle.''

''Which was?''

''I ran a trace on police activity in the area for the night you supposedly died. It wasn't hard to figure out that the Jane Doe who was struck by a car was probably you.''

''No wonder Jeb Parker didn't have any trouble finding me,'' Sara almost cried.

''I went to the clinic, hoping the doctor might be some help. Instead I found Julie.''

There was no mistaking the deep emotion in his tone when he said Julie's name. Sara studied the two of them for only a second. It was obvious their feelings for each other were strong.

''You didn't know she was there?'' Sara asked.

He shook his head. ''I was just hoping she was still alive. I wasn't even sure the ads in the newspaper were from Julie.''

Sara turned to look at Julie, astounded. ''You risked putting ads in the paper for him?''

"It was pure poetry," Julie supplied with a cunning grin.

"Don't you mean purely poetic?" Sara asked.

"No. I mean real poems. Or rather selected lines and verses. See, I knew Dylan's habit of reading the personals, so I discreetly placed ads quoting his favorite poet."

"Dylan Thomas," Sara guessed. "No wonder you're always poring over those books when you sit with the baby. Very sly, Julie. I'm impressed."

"I was desperate," Julie answered. "But let's see what we can do about your predicament."

"I need money and a new identity," she stated. "I've already picked the identity. I've got a few dollars coming my way, but, well, a loan would be great."

"Sara." Julie spoke her name like a warning.

"Just a loan!" she insisted, making a cross over her heart. "I should be able to find work when I pick a town. I've got a bachelor's degree. Double major in hospital administration and information systems. I can repay you in no time."

Julie looked truly disheartened. "Are you sure that's what you want?"

No, I want to stay here with Justin and live happily ever after in this perfect house in this quaint town, working at his clinic and raising his children. "Absolutely. Will you help?"

Julie turned to her friend and he simply nodded.

"Let me see what I can do about the documents. Give me a day or so. The loan is another matter."

"Just bus fare and a few extra dollars," Sara fairly pleaded.

Dylan was smiling at her. It was a charming gesture that helped to quell her uneasiness.

"Tell her," Julie instructed.

"Tell me what?"

Dylan obliged and said, "Violet Mitchum left you a bequest."

"Bequest like in money?" Sara gasped. "But I only met the woman once. Why would she do that?"

"Why don't you ask how much it is?" Julie suggested.

"Okay, how much?"

"One hundred thousand dollars," Dylan proclaimed.

Sara wasn't sure she had heard correctly. "You mean a thousand dollars, right?"

He shook his head. "No, ma'am. There's a hundred grand sitting in an escrow account just waiting for you."

"Why would she do that?" Sara felt stunned, unable to fathom such generosity from a virtual stranger.

"She left you something else, too," Dylan said.

Sara gazed up at him, "More than that huge amount of money? What?"

"Letters."

"Letters?" Sara repeated.

"I'll have them sent down from my office by courier. Julie can find a way to get them to you. Okay?"

"S-sure."

"I have to get back to my baby," Julie said, grabbing Sara's hands. Leaning closer, she whispered a warning. "Think about what you're doing, Sara. Don't make the same mistake I did."

CHAPTER FIFTEEN

"WHO WAS the guy with Julie?" Justin fairly demanded as he walked through the door.

She didn't look up from the journal on internal medicine she'd been perusing. "What are you talking about?"

"The deputy said Julie and a guy came by here. Was it your husband? And why didn't Julie tell me she was coming over here?"

"Maybe she didn't think it was any of your business." She hid her unease behind a laugh.

"Everything about you is my business," Justin insisted.

She willed her brain into overdrive. "Apparently, you scared Julie to death when you were landing the helicopter. She came by to make sure I was okay."

"And the guy?"

"He was...some sort of religious counselor." *Well, it was close to the truth. He had given her hope and a deeper understanding of herself.* "He came to offer me support, if I wanted it."

"Where did Julie find a minister?"

"I didn't ask, but I got the distinct impression that she's turned to this guy for guidance in the past."

Justin was eyeing her suspiciously.

She disarmed him with her brightest smile. "You're getting all worked up over nothing, Justin. It was just a visit from a friend."

"So why didn't she tell me where she was going?"

"Maybe she was afraid you'd tell her not to come."

"I would have," he answered without hesitation. "She should know better than to risk being around you with Jeb Parker on the prowl. I don't want the two of you doing that again."

"Julie and I are both big girls, Justin."

"With big problems," he reminded her.

"Fine, I'll do penance. I'll make you dinner."

"Can you cook?"

"I think I can manage. What do you have in the way of ingredients?"

Justin accompanied her to the fancy refrigerator. It was well stocked. "How about we keep it simple?" he suggested.

"Then it wouldn't be real penance," she informed him. "Back off and allow me to create."

Sara pulled some chicken breasts, lemons and carrots from the fridge. She turned, finding him perched on the barstool, his eyes following her every move.

"Don't you know it isn't polite to stare?" she teased even as she felt the first spark of awareness flicker in her gut.

"I'm not staring. I'm...admiring."

"I don't think I like being *admired* when I cook," she told him. "It makes me feel self-conscious."

"You have nothing to feel self-conscious about," he assured her. His grin was positively lecherous.

"Well, maybe you should feel a little guilty," she said. "Why don't you get off your duff and give me a hand?"

"Where would you like me to give it to you?" he teased as he came around the island and stood next to her.

She lifted her hands, warning him to keep a modest distance. "Remember your rules, Justin." She handed him the bunch of carrots and instructed him to peel and slice them.

"I need flour, wine, some thin pasta and a large pot of water on to boil," she said as she turned to the sink in order to prepare the chicken.

"I'm getting a lot of orders," he grumbled good-naturedly. "Isn't this supposed to be your penance?"

"You know where everything is and I'm not sure I could manage a heavy pot with only one good leg."

"You have two good legs. One just happens to be in a cast for a couple more weeks."

"Are you intentionally trying to bait me?"

His expression fell well short of contrition. "I'm not sure. I just know that I like having you in my kitchen. I like watching you."

She was about to zing him with a one-liner, but found she couldn't. She liked the setup too—the normalcy of preparing a meal in a kitchen with a man adoringly acting as her assistant. It was simple but far from uncomplicated.

She should have been patting the chicken dry, but instead, the full focus of her attention was on him. He stood in a small pantry, reaching up to a high shelf. The action caused the fabric of his shirt to mold against his well-muscled body. That was all she needed to have the spark inside her body burst into a flame.

Maybe it was knowing that she'd be gone in a day or so. Or maybe it was simply that she wanted him beyond reason. It really didn't matter. The end result was the same.

He turned and their eyes locked. It felt like hours passed as they stood little more than a yard apart. Neither one spoke, but communication was real and tangible. She saw her own need mirrored in his eyes. Saw that one hand was tightly clenched at his side.

His mouth was drawn into a thin line and she could almost hear him weighing the pros and cons of his personal dilemma.

She knew she could do something as simple as open the top button of her blouse, but she wouldn't do it. She wanted this to be his decision. He had to make the first move. It was the only way she would be able to leave him with a clear conscience. And leaving was just around the corner.

"It's pointless to pretend I don't want you, isn't it?"

She nodded.

He took a step closer and tossed the box of pasta on the counter. "You were right earlier."

"About what?"

"I don't think of you as married. I know I should, but I don't."

Sara didn't want him to wrestle with that issue. Even if he wouldn't know the whole truth for a few days, or maybe a week, she was not going to put him in that position. On this issue, she could tell him the truth. Or at least a close version of it.

"I spoke to Julie about my divorce this afternoon."

"And?"

She shrugged. "She said some things that got me thinking. So it would be accurate to say that it's a done deal."

He took another step closer. "I'm glad to hear that."

The air between them was charged by an invisible current. It pulled at her like a magnet. "How glad?"

His answer was a slow, sexy smile. "I'll show you."

He came a little closer.

Sara sucked in a jerky breath. "Wait!" she gasped, fighting her own passion for control of her jumbled thoughts.

Justin stilled. He was close enough that she could feel the heat from his body. Close enough that the scent of his now familiar cologne teased her nostrils.

"I'm waiting."

She focused on the third button of his shirt, afraid

that if he really looked into her eyes, he would see the myriad emotions coursing through her. "I need to know what you want from me."

"I've already told you. But if you need to hear it again, I want you."

Not "I love you." That was good, right? That was what she had needed to hear to salve her conscience. She wouldn't be breaking his heart when she left.

It should have made her feel good. Instead, she felt as if she had lost something. Which was stupid. You can't lose something you never had. The best she could salvage from Justin's part in her life was to enjoy the short time they had left.

"Having second thoughts?" he asked, his voice quiet yet tinged with disappointment.

She shook her head, unable to trust her voice. More accurately, she wasn't sure she could keep from telling him how she truly felt. A part of her wanted him to know that he had healed more than her body. He had healed her soul. Thanks to him, she knew she was capable of loving. She had caught a glimpse of what a real relationship should be.

His hand slipped under her chin and he gently lifted her face to his. His eyes scanned her features, his expression registering concern. "Are you afraid that I'll hurt you?"

"Of course not."

"Are we moving too fast? Is that it? I know you still don't have specific memories, but maybe we should wait. I don't want you to regret anything."

She peered up at him as his compassion enveloped her. Waiting was the only thing she *could* regret. Somewhere deep inside her heart, she knew this was her only chance at sampling genuine happiness. After enduring so much, wasn't she entitled to at least one bite of the apple?

"Being with you is what I want," she said, flattening her slightly trembling hands against his strong chest. "No matter what happens in the future, I hope you know that I could never regret you."

"Then dinner will be delayed," he whispered as his mouth covered hers.

She felt him lift her against him. He was carrying her through the house, but she was floating on the sensations brought about by his kiss. Their lips remained sealed as he climbed the steps, then she heard him push a door open with his foot.

Sara found herself in his bedroom. She sensed him everywhere as he placed her in the center of a large, four-poster bed.

She settled her head against the pillow while he yanked each boot off in quick succession. Then he joined her.

His weight caused her to roll to him, nestling her on her side up against his large frame. Justin was feathering kisses against her temple as his fingers traced a path along her spine.

"We have to be careful," he whispered against her hair.

Sara's muddled brain caught on after a minute.

"Right. Contraception will have to be your responsibility."

"Not just that." He chuckled as he pressed her shoulder flat against the mattress. "We have to be careful of your ribs."

She smiled and touched her hand to his cheek. "That isn't the part of my body that aches right now."

He blew out a breath before taking her hand and placing a kiss in her palm. She felt the heat of his mouth as the last rays of sunshine slipped below the horizon.

THE ROOM WAS bathed in the soft glow of dusk. It seemed to add a dreamlike quality to the setting. *Molly was a dream.* Justin reclined on his side, his elbow bent to support his head as he gazed down at her. He had a lock of her hair between the thumb and forefinger of his free hand. "It's so soft," he whispered to her in the shadows, allowing the silky strands to slip from his grasp.

He touched the pulse point of her throat next. First with his fingers, then with his mouth. Her skin tasted of flowers and sweetness. It was a heady combination. He nuzzled against her, teasing her with the tip of his tongue. When she reached for him, Justin caught her hand. He lifted his head long enough to say, "Not yet."

"I want to touch you."

"You will, just give me a little time to explore."

Any further protest was stifled when he covered her mouth and kissed her as softly as his raging body would permit. He wanted this to last. Wanted to savor every second of it.

He shifted again, reaching down to move her injured leg to a safe distance. The muscle in her thigh tensed beneath his touch. His heartbeat was thudding against his chest.

Shadows flickered across the room as he methodically slipped one small button of her blouse free. Her skin was flushed and warm. Her eyes were fixed on his movements.

He slid lower, so that his lips could replace his hands as he continued his slow removal of her clothing. When he kissed the sensitive area around her navel, her hands locked on his shoulders.

For some time he kissed her stomach, enjoying her obvious arousal. He tasted just a hint of saltiness on her flushed warm skin.

At the same time, he lifted his head to look into her eyes, he slipped one finger beneath the waistband of her jeans. She made an incredibly sexy sound as she gasped in a breath.

Once more she attempted to get at his clothing. "Not yet," he whispered.

"Justin?" she pleaded, her tone raspy with desire.

"I want to take my time," he told her, gently kissing the hollow of her throat. "That can't happen if I let you put your hands on me."

"Not fair," she breathed, grabbing a handful of his hair when his mouth closed over her breast.

Taking his finger from her waistband, Justin slipped his hand beneath her and deftly unhooked her bra. With equal efficiency, he held her off the bed just long enough to tug free both her blouse and bra.

He drew one rosy peak into his mouth and teased the other with his fingers. He was vaguely aware that she had called out his name. He continued to kiss and touch her, amazed that his own body hadn't exploded from sheer pleasure.

Sara pulled harder on his hair. It seemed the most expedient way to get his attention. Reluctantly, he lifted his mouth from her skin and she slid her hands to the front of his shirt.

She was trembling so much that her efforts at removing his shirt lacked the finesse and immediacy her body cried out for. Without care or warning, she simply grabbed the material and pulled. The buttons flew, some on the bed, others jingling as they hit the floor.

She didn't care, she was too impatient to wait. Too eager to feel flesh against flesh. Justin didn't comment on her methods. He simply shrugged out of his shirt to allow her access to his body.

His chest was covered in a soft mat of dark hair that tapered in a vee before disappearing into the waist of his jeans. The pads of her fingers followed the path, not stopping when she reached denim.

The fabric was soft, Justin's arousal wasn't. Brazenly, she rubbed him through his clothes and was satisfied and thrilled when she heard him groan against her ear.

Again she experienced that sense of power and control she had never before known. It gave her courage. Allowed her to experience this awakening of her own sexuality. She reached for his belt buckle and, to her utter frustration, found it wasn't a one-handed task.

She started to ease herself up when Justin grasped her hands.

"Let me," he said, kissing her between the words.

Sara watched as he rose off the bed and removed his jeans and his boxers. She felt her eyes widen with appreciation as she gazed upon him. He was magnificent.

"Your turn," he said, moving to the end of the bed.

Sara was astounded that she didn't feel even a twinge of shyness when he slowly worked her pants over the bulk of the cast. He then eased himself between her thighs, until only the flimsy material of her panties separated them.

He held her at the waist as he gave her a long, sensual kiss. Their bodies slipped into a rhythm, heightened by the feel of his erection against her bared stomach.

Sara couldn't wait any longer. She didn't want to wait. It was as if she were standing on the edge of a cliff, ready and eager to jump into a blissful abyss. But she could only make the leap with him inside her.

"Now," she told him. She didn't much care that it came out as a command. She was far too lost in her own longings to care about anything else.

Her eyes flew open when she felt his weight lifting off her. "You're not stopping now, are you?" *Was that really her sounding so desperate?*

"Definitely not," he promised, kissing her briefly before rolling on his side. She heard him open a drawer, followed by the sound of foil being torn.

Foil wasn't the only thing he tore. Justin ripped her panties off at the same time he moved between her legs. Applying gentle pressure, he pushed her thighs apart. The entire time, his eyes never left hers.

She reached up and linked her hands behind his neck, trying to pull him to her.

"I'm too heavy," he explained. "I'm also a little too impatient. I don't want this to hurt you."

His first thrust was tentative and ineffective. She shifted beneath him, sliding her hands down his perspiration-moistened back until she had a firm hold on his incredible derriere. Applying pressure, she arched her hips to meet him.

"Don't," he breathed between tightly clenched teeth.

"I want you," she argued.

"We'll get there. But we're going to do it slowly."

Ignoring him, she tightened her hold. "I don't want slowly."

"I think you'll be sorry," Justin said as his mouth devoured hers.

Sara felt intense pressure and a flash of pain when he entered her. Unable to prevent it, she let out a small cry against his lips.

Justin stilled his body, but his breathing was labored and she could tell his arms were trembling as he held his weight off her.

"I didn't want to hurt you," he said.

She shook her head. She wasn't feeling pain. She felt fulfilled now that her body had adjusted. "I'm not hurt," she promised him, punctuating her remark by with a gentle squeeze. "So don't spoil the moment."

He didn't. He definitely didn't. He seemed to know her body's needs, and when she was close to the edge, he would suddenly change his rhythm, drawing the experience out for a blissful, erotic eternity.

When she felt herself nearing fulfillment yet again, she refused to be denied. "Please?" she begged against his lips. Justin complied, working magic with his hips, and then she was engulfed in sensation as she felt her own release, followed by his.

He moved off her rather quickly, which sounded a silent alarm in her mind. But immediately her concerns were allayed when he pulled her into his embrace. It was several long minutes before she heard his breathing resume a normal rhythm, and she rested her cheek against his chest, listening to the beat of his heart.

This was without question the most amazing experience of her life.

"Thank you," she said in a hushed tone, kissing his warm skin.

"You stole my line," Justin teased. "Did I hurt you?"

"Will you stop asking me that?"

"I can't help it. I'm a doctor. I'm supposed to ask that question."

"I've already answered it. More than twice."

"But I'm well-versed in human anatomy. I should have been more careful. You weren't ready."

"You can be a doctor when we have clothes on," Sara quipped. "When we're like this, just be my lover."

"Fair enough," Justin answered. "Want to take a shower together?"

"And get my cast wet?"

"I forgot," he admitted.

"You go ahead. I'll just lie here basking in the afterglow."

He chuckled, kissed her, then slipped from the bed and went into an adjoining room.

She heard the water come on as she made her first attempt at movement. It was a good thing Justin wasn't there to observe her wince. But she had used muscles she hadn't exercised in years. Her hand skimmed across the sheet, feeling the lingering heat where he had lain with her.

She breathed deeply. His scent was on the pillows. It was comforting. Soothing. So much so that she closed her eyes and dozed off into the first peaceful sleep in a long while.

"WAKE UP."

Sara felt him nudging her shoulder. Reluctantly, she opened her eyes and was astounded to see daylight in the room.

"What time is it?"

"Almost noon," Justin chided with a contented grin. "Should I be offended that you fell asleep, or beat my chest for satisfying you to the point of exhaustion?"

She tossed a pillow at him. "That is such a male thing to say."

"Get up. I've got a surprise for you."

"Breakfast?" she asked, feeling a little ravenous.

"Eventually. You've got thirty minutes to get dressed and come downstairs. I put your bag in the bathroom."

"What's the rush?" she grumbled, not in any hurry to leave his bed.

He cast her an impatient look. "A surprise, by definition, means you aren't forewarned."

"What if I don't like surprises?"

"Trust me," he said as he yanked the warm sheets out of her reach. "This is a surprise that will alter your life forever." He patted her behind. "Get a move on."

When Sara came out of the bathroom, she found a coffee and muffin waiting for her on a tray. She felt positively giddy as she ate and dressed in the allotted time. She dared to hope that Justin's surprise would include saying he loved her before she had to leave.

The giddiness drained from her body. Just the thought of leaving Justin felt like jagged glass slashing her heart into tiny pieces.

She looked at her reflection in the mirror. "I can't leave him." Which left only one option. "I have to tell him the truth. Maybe Julie is right, maybe he'll understand and we can find some way to make a future."

Or he'll walk away from me.

"You've got nothing to lose," she told herself. "If I go ahead with my plans, I leave him behind. If I tell him the truth and he bails out, the result is the same, but at least I'll know I tried. I won't waste time wondering if I made the right decision. Telling the truth, especially after last night, is the only option. I've got a fifty-fifty shot at happiness. Now all I need is to muster up the nerve."

CHAPTER SIXTEEN

"WE HAVE TO TALK," she said in a rush when she reached the bottom of the stairs.

Justin silenced her with a kiss and took her hand. "We will talk," he promised her. "But first, the surprise."

She tried to yank out of his grasp. "Really, Justin. There are some things I need to tell you."

He placed his finger against her lips. "I hate to resort to calling in chits, but I've done a lot for you. Now I'm asking you to do this for me."

"Do what?"

"Be silent and come with me."

"Where?"

"That's part of the surprise."

"But, Justin!" she fairly cried. "I really need to talk."

"Later," he promised, leading her out the door. "And for the record, both verbal and nonverbal communication are acceptable."

"This is important," she insisted.

"Not as important as my surprise. Either come peacefully, or I'll be forced to toss you over my shoulder like a disobedient child and put you in the truck.''

Sara's nerve had been tenuous at best. It was non-existent when she read the determination in his eyes. He was grinning at her with open affection. She might as well enjoy it while it lasted. Besides, what possible difference would it make if she postponed her confession a little while longer?

After helping her climb into the SUV, Justin slipped behind the wheel of his truck, gunned the engine, and headed toward town.

"Where are we going?" she asked when they passed the clinic and made a left.

"You'll see," he answered, revealing nothing. He simply whistled an unnamed tune until he pulled over and parked at the curb in front of the Municipal Center.

"Why are we here?"

"I have something for you."

Since the Municipal Center included a courthouse, she was guessing that his surprise might have something to do with her comment about her divorce being a done deal. What if he expected her to file something legal?

Grabbing his sleeve, she said, "Let's talk before we go inside."

"Just wait." He pulled open the heavy door and ushered her in.

"It can't wait, Justin."

"You're ruining this for me," he warned. "In two

minutes, I promise I'll let you talk to your heart's content.''

"But—''

Too late. She was stepping into the sheriff's office. Alec wasn't alone.

She heard the rattle of metal against metal and looked for the source. A man in an orange jumpsuit was shackled to a chair with his back to her.

"Glad you didn't rush,'' Alec commented dryly.

Justin waved his hand in the direction of the prisoner. "He was picked up in a bar outside Austin last night. Alec arranged to have him brought back here. For starters, he'll be charged with breaking and entering and destruction of property.''

"I don't know what you guys are talking about,'' the prisoner sneered. "I didn't do no B-and-E.''

Sara felt as if she'd been punched. It was impossible for her to take a breath, she was choked by panic and fear.

"Now, Jeb,'' Alec began, using the toe of his boot to shove the chair around, revealing the prisoner's face, "B-and-E is just the beginning. You've stalked and threatened Molly. That will get you—''

"That ain't my Molly,'' the prisoner spat. "I've never seen that bitch before.''

Sara felt Justin drop her hand. She glanced up, trying to read his expression.

"Is he telling the truth?''

She swallowed. "I don't think he's ever seen me, no.''

Justin rubbed his face. "If you know he hasn't seen you, then you must know you're not Molly Parker. What's going on? Has your amnesia been some kind of act?"

She heard the fury behind his accusation. Though she didn't relish the thought of explaining before an audience, she didn't have any choice. "Not at first…" she began, then fearing he would walk away, she spoke quickly. "I woke up at your clinic and you told me I was Molly Parker. It was a couple of days before I remembered who I really was."

"Sara Pierce," Alec interjected.

She ignored Alec, the last thing she needed was his I-told-you-so commentary. "I am Sara Pierce."

Justin let out a string of expletives. "What was your angle?" he demanded.

"Staying alive," she answered with equal force. "I thought I could escape from my ex-husband by becoming someone else. I had no way of knowing that things would mushroom."

"Lies have a way of doing that."

Any guilt she might have felt was overtaken by fierce rage. "How dare you pass judgment on me. I know lying was wrong, but I was out of options. You saw the condition I was in when I was brought to your clinic. I was ready to do anything to keep that animal away from me."

"That doesn't begin to justify what you've done. The people you've put in danger. This Parker guy could have hurt Julie or the baby before he ever realized that he'd been stalking the wrong woman.''

Jeb Parker rattled his shackles. ''To hell with this. I wasn't stalking nobody. And where the hell is my wife?''

Sara turned her eyes on Jeb and wished she could shoot holes through him with her pupils. ''Shut up, you coward! Molly killed herself because she couldn't face the fear of living with a brute like you. She died scared and alone and you're completely to blame for that.''

Parker lashed back with a vulgar suggestion. He turned to Alec and said, ''I ain't done nothing. You got no reason to hold me.''

Alec countered by saying, ''Ignorance is no defense. The fact that you were terrorizing the wrong woman won't affect the charges.''

''Justin?'' Sara pleaded. But when she turned, she discovered that he was gone. And he'd taken her heart with him.

''Wait here,'' Alec said. He took Jeb Parker, struggling and cursing, into a back room.

When he returned, Sara braced herself for the expected berating.

''It was a good plan,'' Alec offered. ''In theory.''

She peered at him through the veil of her lashes. ''I hope you believe that I never intended to involve you or your department in all this.''

Alec shrugged and motioned for her to take a seat.

She sidestepped the one Jeb had been shackled to and sank into the other.

"Am I going to be charged with filing false reports?"

"No." He spun his chair around, poured two cups of coffee, then handed one to her. "Cream, sugar?"

"Arsenic," she grumbled.

Alec surprised her by chuckling at her morbid remark. "I was telling Parker the truth. The fact that he didn't realize you weren't his wife won't mitigate things in court."

Her shoulders slumped. "I can't stick around for court."

"Sara, you have to. Parker belongs in jail."

She held his gaze. "I know that better than you do, Sheriff."

"Alec," he corrected.

"But the minute word gets out that I'm alive, my ex-husband will come after me. Unlike Molly Parker, I don't want to die."

"I can hold Parker for forty-eight hours. After that, I'll need some evidence to take to the prosecutor."

"I don't have any," Sara said. "Molly Parker was mumbling incoherently when I met her at the shelter."

"Did she say her husband had beaten her?"

Sara tried to recall. "I don't know. Maybe."

"And you never saw him before today?"

She shook her head. "Can't you use phone records

to prove he called me at the guesthouse before he went there?''

"Nope. The incoming call was from a cell phone. Untraceable."

"What about the note, or the paint or fingerprints? Isn't there any physical evidence? He doesn't seem bright enough to pull off a flawless crime."

"We're still waiting to hear back on the prints, but don't hold your breath. Even the stupid ones get lucky. So what are you going to do?"

Sara's smile was a polite gesture, not a genuine reflection of her feelings. "I need to stay in Cactus Creek for a day or so. Julie has already agreed to help me."

Alec's expression was as dark as the strong coffee steaming in the cup. "You told Julie the truth?"

Sara nodded. "Yesterday."

"Then why weren't you honest with Justin?"

"Believe it or not, I tried to tell him this morning."

"Why?"

"Excuse me?"

"Why were you going to tell him the truth?"

"He's been wonderful to me. He deserved to know."

"That's the reason?"

Sara eyed Alec, carefully considering her answer. "I'm in love with him."

If Alec had an opinion about her confession, he didn't let on. "Did you tell him that?"

"No."

"Planning on doing it before you leave town?"

"No. Besides, I doubt he'd believe anything I said now."

"You're probably right," Alec agreed, confirming her worst fear. "What if I need you to put Jeb Parker behind bars?"

She shoved her hair off her face. "I hope you won't. But I'll agree to let you know where to find me once I relocate. I'd like you to agree that you'll only use me as a last resort."

"Fair enough. You want me to see if I can track Justin down?"

"It would be pointless. Can I call Julie?"

"Be my guest," Alec said, passing her the phone.

"MEN CAN BE such fools," Julie groused when they opened the room Sara had rented.

"I dug my own hole," Sara told her friend. "This place could use a good airing out."

"It's a boardinghouse," Julie reminded her. "And I believe I suggested you let me take you to a hotel in the city. It isn't as if you're strapped for cash anymore."

"It's fine for a night or two," Sara insisted. Sadness weighed heavily on her when Julie placed the small duffel bag on the unmade bed. "Justin didn't waste any time tossing my things to the curb, did he?"

"Justin is lucky I didn't toss him to the curb," Julie

stated. "There is nothing more infuriating than a man drowning in his own self-righteousness."

"It isn't self-righteousness," Sara defended. "He's angry and he has every right to be."

'He should get over it. I told him exactly that when he came to the clinic with your bag."

"Don't waste your breath," Sara insisted. "It's more than just the lies."

"You actually think that because you slept with him he is entitled to be pigheaded?"

"Who said I slept with him?"

Julie rolled her eyes. "Nobody had to say it. It was a foregone conclusion. The guy is in love with you. You're in love with him. It was bound to happen."

"This information about him loving me came to you in a dream?" Sara asked.

"Fine," Julie huffed. "Be as hardheaded as Justin. He made a rude remark when I told him how you felt, too."

· "You shouldn't have done that."

"Tell me it isn't true and I'll never mention it again."

Sara looked away but remained silent.

"I swear, the two of you should be locked in a room together until you're forced to work this out."

"The only thing I have to work out is leaving Cactus Creek," Sara insisted. "Preferably without seeing Justin again."

"Dylan went back late yesterday. He's going to

send a cashier's check when he has all the documents ready."

"Thank him for me."

"I did." Julie turned toward the door, paused and said, "The letters from Violet Mitchum arrived this morning. I put them in your bag."

At least they would give her something to do, Sara mused once she was alone in her room. Something that would keep her from thinking about Justin.

Opening the bag, she found a stack of letters tied with a neat, faded pink ribbon. On top was a brief note from Dylan explaining that her only obligation was to attend a memorial service for Violet. He'd contact her with the details when everything was worked out.

Sara had no idea what it would be like to have financial freedom. Especially when the money came from such an unexpected source. A hundred thousand dollars could put a lot of distance between her and Hank Allen. Oddly, that seemed to pale in comparison with the knowledge that she'd also be relegating Justin to her memory.

"This is too ironic," she breathed. "First I have no money and a lousy life. Now I have money and a lousy life. I guess you can't buy happiness."

She undid the ribbon around the letters. The paper had long since yellowed, but a trace of perfume still clung to the old pages.

The postmarks began during World War II. Sara lay across the bed, picturing Violet sitting down to write her soldier husband. Her hair would be perfectly styled and she would be wearing a tailored dress, listening to a big-band record through the scratchy speaker of an old Victrola.

The letter was tender and chatty. It seemed as if Violet had taken great pains to tell her absent husband every detail of her day-to-day existence. She even described the foods she was canning and lamented the inconvenience of ration stamps. Mostly, she told her beloved Charlie how empty she felt with him so far away.

"I can relate to that," Sara mused.

The next letter was written in a bold, masculine hand. Charlie gushed appreciation for her daily letters, even though they were taking some time to catch up with him. He wasn't at liberty to tell her where he was or what he was doing, but he promised her that he would return to her soon.

Sara wiped a tear from her face as she continued to read the back and forth communication that spanned more than a year. She had a clear picture of the two of them in her mind. Violet was patiently, if anxiously, awaiting his return, knitting baby clothes for the houseful of children they discussed in almost every letter. Charlie was brave and patriotic. He believed in the war he was helping to win. He often wrote that knowing Violet was waiting for him was what helped him stay sane during the horrors of battle.

"No wonder you felt comfortable giving me advice

in the hospital," Sara said out loud. "You and Charlie lived a fairy tale."

However, the next letter in the stack shattered that notion. Unlike the others, this was a single sheet, and Charlie had only written two lines. Sara read them aloud. "I've been wounded. Get a divorce."

She had to reach for the lamp since it had grown dark during her hours of reading. She immediately opened Violet's response. It was equally brief. She didn't care if he was wounded and she wouldn't ever give him a divorce.

There didn't seem to be a response from Charlie. The next letter was also penned by Violet. It was long and direct. Sara smiled as she read the neatly written words. Violet had contacted the Army and knew her husband was aboard a hospital ship headed for Virginia. She was going to meet him there, sewing basket in hand, and if he even mentioned the word *divorce* to her, she was going to sew his mouth shut.

Charlie answered that letter. In painful detail, he explained to Violet that his wound had left him unable to give her the children they had planned. He wasn't going to cheat her out of the family she wanted. Charlie was a kind man. He was also smart. He never once came right out and used the word *divorce*.

The last letter was dated in the late eighties. Violet's handwriting was tremulous but her sentiments were still as clear as ever. She was writing a farewell letter to the man who had been her husband for almost fifty years. Apparently he was in the hospital and Violet was at his side. She knew he was dying. Instead of succumbing to her impending grief, she wrote of how happy her life had been. How much she had enjoyed building the ranch, working side-by-side with Charlie. Later, they had traveled the world together. The last thing Violet wrote was to remind her husband of how close they had come to missing out on such a full and happy marriage. Children would have been welcomed, but she never once regretted not having them. Because she had him. His unconditional love and devotion were more than any woman could have wanted.

Sara reached for a tissue from the nightstand. She felt kind of silly, sitting in a musty room crying like a baby. But the letters had touched her, spoken to her.

She was sure Violet had intended her to read the letters when she was still trapped in her abusive marriage. The kindly old woman had probably hoped that reading them would convince Sara to free herself to search for real love.

Ironically, she was being taught a different lesson. A more important one. Real love was worth fighting for. Just as Violet had refused to let Charlie go without a fight, Sara wasn't going to do that with Justin, either.

She just had to find a plan that would work. She was about to start formulating that plan when she heard a knock on the door. "Just a second!" she called, dabbing the last few teardrops from her eyes.

She allowed herself to hope it might be Justin. Braced for that possibility, she opened the door.

A scream died in her throat as Hank Allen grabbed her by the hair and yanked her off the floor.

CHAPTER SEVENTEEN

"THOUGHT I MIGHT find you here," Alec said.

"Back off," Justin warned, nursing another sip of beer.

His friend said nothing, but he did plop down on the stool next to his and order a scotch, neat.

When Alec reached for the glass, he dropped a file on the bar. Curiosity got the better of Justin, so he asked, "What's this?"

"I did a little checking on Sara Pierce."

"Good for you."

"Interesting stuff."

"I doubt it."

"Read for yourself," Alec suggested.

Justin countered with a rather graphic suggestion of where Alec could stick the file. His pager went off so he glanced down at the number. It was from Julie, a code of numbers they had agreed upon. He pressed a button to silence the beep and clear the display.

"Emergency?" Alec queried.

"Nope. It's Julie."

"How can you be so sure nothing's wrong? What about her baby?"

"I just checked him. He's fine. Besides, we both

know why Julie is paging me. I've got to admit, I'm surprised at you.''

''Why?'' Alec asked.

Justin wasn't buying his friend's relaxed, conversational tone. ''You warned me about Mol—*Sara*. You haven't been one of her biggest fans.''

''True. But I'm man enough to admit when I'm wrong.''

''Great, you can go on *Oprah*—a perfect example of the sensitive guy.''

''You got it bad,'' Alec chuckled softly.

''Bad enough to want to punch something. Wanna volunteer?''

Alec held up his hands. ''Hear me out, then, if you still feel like hitting me, I'll give you the first punch for free.''

''We aren't kids anymore,'' Justin scoffed. He and Alec had often settled things with their fists. No one ever got hurt; it was just a way of getting whatever was bothering them out of their systems. His pager beeped again. ''Forget it, Julie,'' he grumbled. He turned and met his friend's eyes. ''Since I'm being ganged up on, say what you have to say and then leave me alone.''

''She tried playing it by the rules, Doc.''

''Right,'' Justin jeered. ''I saw firsthand how she manipulated us. I doubt she knows how to face anything honestly.''

''You can be a real horse's ass, know that?''

''Thanks.''

"The guy she was married to—"

"Are you so sure she's divorced?"

"Shut up for a minute, Justin. Or I'll be the one throwing the first punch."

"Fine." Justin took another sip of beer.

"Sara was married to a guy who owns a string of pretty successful gyms. But he preferred to use her as a punching bag."

"Then she should have left." Justin hated himself for saying something so callous.

"She did. She filed police reports. Had him arrested. He even spent some time in jail because she testified against him in court. We both know how hard it is for an abused woman to face her batterer in court."

Justin heard himself ask, "So what happened?"

"She moved away, got a divorce." Alec's tone was a blend of respect and amusement. "Get this, she nailed him for alimony *and* he was ordered to pay her college tuition."

"Good for her."

"Not good enough," Alec said. "She got her degree a month ago. Apparently, her ex decided to give her a graduation present."

"A beating?" Justin asked, though he already knew the answer. He'd seen the results. "Sounds like a prince of a guy."

"One of her neighbors called the cops. He bolted before they arrived. She refused medical treatment at the scene, then must have grabbed the first bus out of town.''

''That's all admirable, Alec, but it doesn't explain why she would lie to me. To us.''

''When did you get stupid, Doc?'' Alec drawled. ''She was shafted by the system.''

''So she stole the identity of some poor dead woman?''

''She was handed an opportunity and she took it,'' Alec corrected. ''It was the smart play.''

''Maybe in the beginning,'' Justin relented. He cursed when Julie paged him for the third time. ''Believe me, she had plenty of opportunities to tell me the truth. I was her doctor. If she's as smart as you claim, she must have known anything she said would be confidential.''

''You stopped being *just* her doctor a long time ago,'' Alec said.

''Do I get my free punch now?'' Justin demanded.

Alec downed his drink and put the glass on the bar with a thud. ''If you think it will make you feel better.''

The chirp of a pager sounded again, and automatically, Justin reached for his. But it was Alec who was being called.

''It's the clinic,'' he told Justin.

''I'm sure Julie is trying to find me through you.''

''I'll check it out,'' Alec said, slipping from the stool.

As soon as Alec had disappeared around the corner

of the bar to use the phone, Justin reached for the file. He flipped it open and started reading the faxed cover page. It sickened him to see the extent of the abuse Sara had suffered at the hands of her ex-husband. It was a laundry list of incidents dating from just after her marriage.

He couldn't stand it so he closed the file. Alec had been right. He was being an ass. Sara didn't deserve his anger. If anything, she was entitled to his compassion. Most of all, he hoped it wasn't too late to offer his love.

After tossing some bills on the bar, he turned to leave but was intercepted by Alec. He knew something was wrong in an instant. Guilt washed over him. "Please tell me the baby is okay?" He never should have ignored the page.

"It isn't the baby," Alec said. "It's Sara. She's gone."

"Where?"

"Mrs. Lawson from the boardinghouse called Julie a little while ago. She said a man had come in and left with Sara. She's pretty sure Sara didn't want to go."

Justin felt his heart explode.

"Was it good?" Hank Allen taunted. "I know you spent the night with him."

Sara willed every muscle in her body to remain still. She didn't want to do anything to antagonize

Hank Allen. Especially not now. Not when he was holding her hostage in Justin's house.

"He's a doctor," she answered. She tried to put just enough fear in her voice to make him feel powerful.

Hank Allen gripped her throat and squeezed. She saw dark spots and wondered if she would lose consciousness again. He liked that. It was one of his favorite tortures.

He let go with a jerk and she coughed as she gulped in air. She felt moisture on her cheeks, but it wasn't until she tasted salty tears that she realized she was crying.

Clearing her throat, she said, "Let's leave here. I'll go home with you."

He slapped her. "What makes you think I want you now?"

He glared at her with raw hatred in his eyes as he paced around the living room. She followed his movements with her eyes, wondering if he would notice the gun resting on the mantel. Praying he wouldn't. Why hadn't she picked it up, kept it within reach as Justin had instructed?

Hank Allen sheathed and unsheathed the hunting knife strapped to his thigh. Sara was well acquainted with the weapon. He had held it to her throat on many occasions.

"Where is your new boyfriend?" he asked.

Sensing his growing impatience, Sara tried to use it to her advantage. "He had to go to a medical conference. He's going to be away for a while. That's why I took a room in town.''

"Liar!"

She braced for a blow that thankfully didn't happen. "He isn't my boyfriend, Hank Allen. I swear."

"Fine," he growled. "Then you won't care when I cut him into pieces. You can watch, then it will be your turn."

Bile rose in her throat. "Don't do this. I'll go with you. Do whatever you want. The doctor isn't part of this."

"Sure he is," Hank Allen hissed. "He had you. I can see it in your eyes so don't even think of denying it. He'll pay for putting his hands on you. Then you'll pay for letting him."

"How can there be no trace of them?" Justin screamed.

Alec turned from the fax machine, his expression grim. "It's worse than we thought."

"How could it get worse?"

"We got a print match on a partial that was lifted from your guesthouse. Hank Allen Pierce."

Justin raked his hands through his hair. "He's been stalking her? How?"

"This is from a body shop near Hank Allen's house." Alec passed him the still-warm fax. "Front-end damage. I'm sure we can match the paint chips we found at the scene."

"He ran her down three weeks ago?" Just asking the question chilled Justin to the core.

"Apparently," Alec agreed. "He must have been following her all along."

"Why? What will it take to get this maniac out of her life?"

"A coffin."

Justin glared at his friend. "That's encouraging."

"I'm trying to prepare you, Doc. This is one determined psycho. I've got every officer in the area on alert, but no one has seen them. They haven't had time to reach the interstate, but I've arranged for roadblocks just in case they make it that far."

Justin scratched his head, his mind racing along with his heart. "I'm going home to get my gun. I'll hunt the bastard down myself."

"Don't be stupid, Doc. You should probably lay low for a while. If he knows about you and Sara, he might come after you, too."

Justin and Alec locked eyes. "Has anyone checked my house?"

"Why would he take Sara to your place?"

"It would explain why no one has spotted his car!" Justin thundered.

"Well, if he did take her there, he did it for one reason."

"Hey, he wants a piece of me, fine."

Justin turned and bolted for the door. He heard and ignored Alec just behind him. Taking the steps three at a time, he reached his car and shoved Alec aside.

He left with a squeal of burning rubber drowning out Alec's protests.

. He made it back to his house in record time. There was no sign of anything amiss, but it wouldn't have altered his determination if Hank Allen had been standing at the door with a rifle trained on his chest.

Justin put his key in the lock, all his senses on alert. Pushing the door open, he saw Sara on the sofa just as she screamed to warn him off.

His fury was fueled when he saw the vivid red marks on her throat and the bruise on her cheek.

In a flash, a man dressed in black leaped up, pulling Sara with him. Sunlight glinted off the knife blade pressed at her throat.

"Leave, Justin," Sara pleaded.

"Do it and I'll slit her throat."

He took a long look at Hank Allen. The man was bulked muscle and blind rage.

"Please?" he heard her beg softly. "Get out, Justin."

Her captor yanked her by the hair, swinging her around as if she were a rag doll. "Shut up!" Hank Allen warned Sara, pressing the knife deeper into her skin. "You!" he called to Justin, "come join us. I knew you'd show up sooner or later."

Sara cried out when her hair was yanked yet again.

"That was for lying," Hank Allen seethed. He looked up at Justin. "She told me you were away at some convention. Now, why do you think my wife lied?"

Justin shrugged. "She didn't. I had some patients to see. I just came home to pack."

He was standing just a few feet from the gun cabinet, but knew any attempt to retrieve a weapon might end up getting Sara killed.

"Get in here," Hank Allen instructed. "If I have to say it again, I'll get angry. Ask my wife what happens when I get angry."

"No need," Justin said, struggling to keep his voice calm. "Okay, I'm here. Why don't you let her go?"

"Isn't that sweet, Sara?" he hissed against her ear. "Your boyfriend is willing to throw down his life for yours."

Justin's eyes met hers, silently offering comfort. But she knew all too well what her ex was capable of. She had to get Justin out of there. She mouthed the word *leave* but he ignored her. She did it again, with the same result. There was only one thing she could think to do. She only hoped she lived through it.

"That's because he's more of a man than you are, Hank Allen—aahhh!" She choked out the strangled cry when his fist jabbed into her ribs.

"Be quiet, Sara," Justin urged.

"Why?" she continued through the pain. "He knows it's the truth. He beats on me because he's too much of a wimp to go toe-to-toe with—" Her words were cut off when Hank Allen threw her to the floor.

Sara's chest felt as if it were on fire. She turned her head in time to see Justin lunging over the sofa.

She saw the blade of the knife slash Justin's hand as the two men tumbled to the ground. Justin was bigger, but Hank Allen was strong.

Placing her hand on the hearth, she eased herself up, feeling the pain of her lung deflating. Justin was doing an admirable job of fending off Hank Allen's attempts to cut him. But his hand was bleeding profusely and she guessed it was only a matter of time before Justin weakened.

The gun was her only hope and she was determined to use it. She clawed her way up the stone fireplace. She reached up with her arm, groping on the mantel until she finally felt the cold metal barrel.

She fell, but she had managed to bring the gun down with her. With what felt like her last drop of energy, she lifted the gun off the floor and tried to hold it steady.

Everything began to fade, she was losing consciousness. The two men were little more than a blur of twisted images. Sara focused on his black shirt and squeezed the trigger. She didn't last long enough to hear the sound of the shot. Wasn't sure she actually fired before darkness claimed her.

EPILOGUE

"FINALLY."

It took incredible effort for Sara to open her eyes. Tears immediately blurred her vision when she saw Justin standing over her. He bent down and brushed her lips with a kiss.

"Your arm?" she said as soon as she noticed the sling. The hand sticking out of the sling was heavily bandaged as well. "What happened?"

"Stay still," he instructed, smoothing her hair as he sat on the edge of her bed.

She felt a tight sensation on her side and started to reach for it.

"It's a chest tube," he explained. "They had to reinflate your lung. It was punctured when Hank Allen fractured your rib."

"Did he cut you badly?" she asked.

"I'll have an ugly scar on my left hand. Think you can live with that?"

"And your shoulder?"

Justin smiled down at her. "You did that."

"What?"

"You shot me."

Sara was dumbstruck.

"I'll have a scar there, too. But you missed all the important things."

"I sh-shot you?"

"Flesh wound," he answered, grinning.

"I didn't mean for you to get hurt," she protested. "I'm so sorry, Justin."

He started laughing.

"You think this is funny?"

"Actually, I do. It will be a great story to tell our grandchildren."

She shrank back. "I'm a little lost here. The last thing I remember was you and Hank Allen fighting."

"You do seem to have persistent memory problems. Seems to me, we're pretty much back where we started."

She scowled at him. "From the beginning, Justin. Tell me everything."

"You shot me."

"I heard that part. How did you get away from Hank Allen?"

His expression darkened. "Alec took care of him."

"Is he in jail?"

Justin shook his head and quietly fixed his gaze on her. "He's dead, Sara."

She let out a breath. She couldn't remember when Hank Allen hadn't been a threatening dark cloud hanging over her life. She had married the man, yet hearing he was dead left her feeling nothing but complete relief.

"Do you want some time alone?" Justin asked.

She gaped at him. "To do what?"

"Mourn...think?"

Now it was her turn to laugh. Justin's noble effort in making the offer fell ridiculously short of sincere. "Why would I need to mourn a pig like him?"

"You were married to him," Justin said. His expression seemed to drain of humor. He looked utterly serious when he asked, "I'll understand if you need time and space."

Crooking her finger, she got him to lean close enough for her to take his shirt into her fist. "Don't you know that you're all I need? Haven't you figured that out yet?"

His smile stole her breath. "What about kids?"

"What about them?"

"I want some," he said as he brushed her lips with a kiss.

"How many is some?"

"Up to you."

"When do you want these kids?"

"Soon."

Sara kissed him. "What if we don't have children?"

He stared down at her, looking utterly confused. "What are you asking?"

"I'm asking what would happen if we couldn't have children for some reason."

"What's the reason?"

"It's a hypothetical question, Justin. Answer me."

"It wouldn't matter. We'd have each other."

"Good answer," she said. "Are we having these children out of wedlock?"

She felt his smile against her mouth. "Are you asking me to marry you?"

"It would be prudent, if we're having children."

He lifted his head. "What if we don't have children?"

She sighed. "I want to have children with you, Justin."

"Okay. But what if it doesn't happen?"

"Then I'll have you."

"So will you marry me?"

Smiling, she answered, "No."

His brows arched. "You don't want to marry me?"

"I didn't say that."

"You refused my proposal."

"Because you left out an important element."

"Which was?"

"You haven't told me you loved me yet."

"How could I not love you? After all, you shot me."

Sara smiled. "Good point, then I accept."

"But I'm taking back my proposal."

"Why?"

"I think you know."

"I love you, Justin."

He kissed her with a tenderness that almost brought her to tears. Sara knew in her soul that she had found true happiness.

Silently, she said, "Thank you, Violet."

TRUEBLOOD, TEXAS
continues next month with
HOT ON HIS TRAIL
by Karen Hughes

Matt Radcliffe had a lot at stake, leading an old-fashioned cattle drive out of New Mexico. He didn't have time for pesky Calley Graham, an investigator who insisted on dragging him back to Pinto, Texas. But Calley figured if she volunteered to take over as a camp cook, she could keep her job, and maybe get to keep the cowboy, too!

Here's a preview!

CHAPTER ONE

MATT TURNED TO CALLEY. "Is there a problem?"

"Yes. And I think it's you."

He pointed to the east, where the sun was barely peeking over the horizon, "It's almost time to break camp. The boys are ready. The cattle are ready. Hell, even the mules look ready. The only thing that isn't ready is you."

"Is that why you bit Boyd's head off?"

A muscle flexed in his jaw. "I think you're distracting my crew."

She reached for the coffeepot and poured him a cup. "And I think you're suffering from an empty stomach and not enough sleep."

"I wish it was that simple," he muttered, then took the cup from her and blew on the steaming coffee. "Maybe we should start over."

"Okay," she said with a smile. "Good morning, Matt."

He gave her a reluctant smile. "Good morning, Calley."

She lifted the lid off the Dutch oven. "Breakfast is ready if you're hungry."

"I'm starved." But he wasn't looking at the food

she dished up. He was looking at her. Then the rest of the crew ambled over to the campfire and Matt turned and took a seat on one of the crates.

Calley dished up full plates for everyone, serving herself last. Pride welled up within her after she took the first bite.

"It's delicious," she announced, unable to keep the surprise out of her voice.

Everyone else was too busy chewing to reply. For the first time, Calley believed she might be able to pull this off.

"Let's roll out," Matt said, handing her his empty plate.

"I need to wash dishes first." She removed the Dutch oven and coffeepot from the crate.

"There's no time," he replied. "You can do it when we make camp tonight."

She frowned down at the scorch marks in the bottom of the Dutch oven. "Do you have any idea how hard this pot and the rest of these dishes will be to clean by then?"

"That's not my problem." A hopeful gleam lit his eyes. "It won't be your problem, either, if you decide to go back where you came from."

Calley had known from the beginning that Matt didn't want her here, but his remark stung anyway. She'd wanted to prove to him she could handle this job. *Any job*. Obviously, it was going to take more than one good breakfast to do it.

She forced a smile. "That's all right. I'll manage."

''Suit yourself.''

He walked away and Calley had to resist the urge to throw the coffeepot at his head. She was probably just tired, too. Sleeping in a strange bedroll, on the hard floor of a strange chuck wagon, in a strange state, wasn't exactly conducive to a good night's sleep.

But it was the most excitement she'd had in a very long time.

Calley dumped the dirty dishes in an empty crate, then hauled it to the chuck wagon. After she'd gathered all her supplies, she reached for her purse and dug out the prescription bottle she'd carried with her for too many years to remember. She popped the familiar red-and-white capsule into her mouth, then washed it down with the last of her lukewarm coffee.

She had no intention of letting a bunch of dirty dishes, a cantankerous cowboy, or a bum heart keep her from having the time of her life.

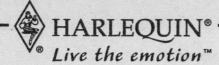

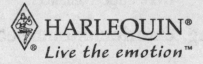

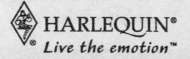

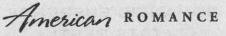
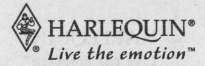

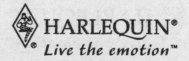